"I thought we made a good team tonight."

It had been a long time since she felt like she belonged anywhere, let alone on a team. Adrian was one of the true good guys. With his profile to her, she could study his features. He was still good-looking, and the years added maturity and depth. She didn't really understand why he was still single.

He put his hands into the front pockets of his worn-just-right jeans. With a quick turn of his head, he glanced at her before looking back to the sky. "Anyway, I was wondering if you liked live music." He looked down. "Mia is going to her first sleepover since the accident." He took a deep breath. "So I was wondering if you would want to go to Kerrville with me. A friend from the bull-riding days is playing at a restaurant, and I thought going there would be better than sitting alone and worrying about Mia. Would you want to go with me?"

"Are you asking me on a date?"

A seventh-generation Texan, **Jolene Navarro** fills her life with family, faith and life's beautiful messiness. She knows that as much as the world changes, people stay the same. Vow-keepers and heartbreakers. Jolene married a vow-keeper who shows her holding hands never gets old. When not writing, Jolene teaches art to inner-city teens and hangs out with her own four almost-grown kids. Find Jolene on Facebook or her blog, jolenenavarrowriter.com.

Books by Jolene Navarro

Love Inspired

Lone Star Legacy
Texas Daddy

Lone Star Holiday
Lone Star Hero
A Texas Christmas Wish
The Soldier's Surprise Family

Love Inspired Historical

Lone Star Bride

Texas Daddy

Jolene Navarro

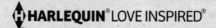

LOVE INSPIRED BOOKS

Recycling programs
for this product may
not exist in your area.

ISBN-13: 978-0-373-89948-7

Texas Daddy

www.Harlequin.com

Printed in U.S.A.

Rejoice always, pray continually,
give thanks in all circumstances;
for this is God's will for you in Christ Jesus.
—*1 Thessalonians* 5:16–18

To My Sisters

Tracye Ward and Amanda Warren

Through times of joy, tribulations, grief and happiness you have been there. As different as we are, we are also the same. Love you.

Acknowledgments

First, foremost and always with all my heart, thank you to my hero, my husband, Fred Navarro. He gave me the time I needed to pull this story together and has been known to do the dishes without even being asked.

Thank you to Alexandra Sokoloff, Linda Trout, Carol Green Kiar, Laura Stephens, Gail Hart, Jenna Neal, Vaun Murphrey, Melody Robinette, Linda Fry, Deann Alford Landers and the West Texas Writer's Academy class of 2015 for brainstorming this story. Plotting is always more fun with a group.

To my writer friends of San Antonio Romance Authors. You are an endless source of inspiration. Teri Wilson, Patricia Walters-Fischer, Lupe Gonzalez, Mary Brand, Manie Culver, Suanne Schefer, Willa Blair, Ani Stubs, Curtis Copley, Troy Bernhardt, Joni Hahn and Pamla Morsi. Just to name a few.

To Storm Navarro and Sasha Summers for everything.

And to Emily Rodmell, my editor, and Pam Hopkins, my agent. Thank you for taking the stories I have in my dyslexic brain and helping me polish them to be the best they can be.

Thank you for this dream of being a Harlequin author.

Chapter One

The rain dripped off the edge of his Stetson as Adrian De La Cruz surveyed the overgrown terrain for stray cattle. The mare moved forward with sure steady steps, her ears twisting back and forth letting him know she was on the lookout also. He enjoyed riding in a light drizzle. An angry bolt of lightning struck at the hills.

Well, the weather report had got it wrong. The problem? He was too far in the old Cortez place to make it back to the Childress's barns.

Thunder rolled through the valley. Lying low over Zeta's neck, he pushed her into a full run on the weed-covered road. His eyes stung as the wind bit into exposed skin. A series of lightning strikes hopped across the clouds, joined by a chorus of rumbles.

Adrenaline flooded his body. Over ten years

ago he would have sat up and laughed at the sky, consumed by a need to test his limits.

He couldn't afford such recklessness. His daughter needed him to come home in one piece, especially now. He closed his eyes just long enough to clear the image of her boot trapped in the stirrup. He hadn't been fast enough to stop the damage to her leg.

Mud flew as the powerful strides of his mare ate the earth. Moments like this, he missed the rush of excitement as he sat on two thousand pounds of unpredictable bull and waited for the gate to be pulled.

Thunder rattled the Texas Hill Country and a flash of blinding light revealed the old cabin on the left side of the abandoned country path. In one motion, Zeta slid to a stop and he dismounted. The shed attached to the rustic cabin looked leak-free, the dirt floor dry. The discarded crates and boxes were old but in good shape.

Loosening Zeta's girth, he laughed as she shook like a dog. She tossed her head in a way to let him know she wasn't happy and scowled at him for being irresponsible.

"I know." He patted her neck. "We'll hang here until the storm passes. Shouldn't be long." He pulled his phone out, only to find it had died. He'd forgotten to charge it again.

School would be out soon. He removed his hat and shook off the rain. Ugh. It didn't look like he would get back in time to pick Mia up. At least his brother, George, would get his daughter if he was a no-show. The rain hit the old metal roof hard.

Maybe there was a landline inside the cabin. Dashing to the covered porch, he caught sight of an odd figure coming toward the cabin from the opposite side of the ravine.

He stepped closer to the edge of the steps. Someone in a fluorescent green jacket was trying to walk across the field. They carried a bike, each step lumbering and uneven. His eyes narrowed trying to make out if the mud-covered body belonged to a man or woman.

Probably some crazy adventure-seeking city slicker lost. They seemed to think fences were for jumping. They had to be trespassing.

It wasn't an easy ranch to get to, and Bergmann had locked it down after his wife had been killed in an accident on this very road.

Pulling his hat low, he charged into the rain to help. Halfway out, he knew without a doubt it was a woman. One mystery solved. When he got closer, the problem became clear. The chains of the bike were tangled with a large metal knee brace she wore on her right leg. The brace covered less of her leg than his daughter's, but it had the same knee hinge. One of her hands held the mangled bike while the other wrapped around her middle in an awkward way. Each step looked like a struggle.

Thunder warned of the next flash of light. He went to her left side to help her move faster. At first she shoved him back with her shoulder, or tried to at least.

"Let me help you. I work on the neighboring ranch. I'm—"

"Adrian De La Cruz. I remember you. Thanks, but I've got this." She blew at the hair that hung in her eyes, but the effort didn't move the muddy mess. "You're working for Childress now?" she managed between gritted teeth.

He moved forward, trying to put the puzzle pieces together. He had to know her. Most people outside of family and close friends couldn't tell him and his twin apart. With a growl, she yanked at the twisted bike again.

"I hate to admit it, but I think I do need help." She looked at him, her light blue eyes as endless as a clear summer sky.

Then it hit him.

"Nikki Bergmann?" He hadn't seen the oldest Bergmann sister in over twelve years. Back when he went to all the girls' basketball games just to watch her play. He pretended to be there for his sisters, but his attention was all on her.

"I didn't know you were back in town." Shocking, considering around here people told everyone's business before they even knew what was happening themselves, and half the time it was wrong.

Just yesterday he had been at her family hardware store, and her sisters hadn't said a thing.

With a scowl, she pulled at her brace. Rain started coming down so hard the hills around them vanished from sight. The bump around her middle moved. Under closer inspection, he could see she had some kind of small animal tucked in her jacket.

Crazy woman. This was getting ridiculous. His sisters made sure he had been raised to respect women, but he wasn't going to stand out here waiting to be fried while she battled her ego. And he couldn't leave her.

"Let me get the bike off you." Without waiting for her permission, he flipped the chain on its side and snapped the joints. Pulling the ruined bike free of the broken chain, he tossed it aside.

He put one arm under hers and ran for the cabin. She gave a few objections, but she didn't refuse his help this time. "What kind of critter do you have hidden away?" His daughter had a habit of saving baby animals. What was it with females and babies? Well, not all females. Mia's mother had left without a single hug or smile for their newborn daughter.

Nikki grunted, interrupting the dark turn of his thoughts. They arrived at the steps of the porch, and the sound became a low frustrated growl. Her muscles bunched with tension. "I can't get my leg high enough to make the step."

"I'll pick you up." He bent to scoop her up. At first she was stiff. "I'm just going to put you on the porch." With a nod, he felt her fit muscles soften.

The bundle squirmed again, and she giggled, sounding like a young girl for a moment. He remembered her being the serious older sister. They had lost their mother young, and Nikki had taken on the responsibility of mothering her younger twin sisters. Everyone knew their stepmother had been no help and left them with a half sister to raise.

She pulled away and he almost lost his balance. "Easy, Bergmann. Is it still Bergmann?" He tried to ease her to the boards as she struggled to stand on her own.

She grabbed his arm and nodded. He wasn't sure if it was to save him from falling or to keep herself upright. He did like the idea that she wasn't married.

"Here, sit on the bench. So what do you have there?" He tried to peek in, but she was zipped up all the way to her neck. "Give it to me and then we can get you untangled from that brace."

She had to sit at an odd angle to accommodate her leg trapped in the mangled brace. The hinge was locked. Once settled, she pushed her hood back.

For a moment he forgot to breathe. Her face was so much like the young teen he adored, but deeper, more lived in, more beautiful than he remembered. He had been fascinated with her.

Now, as a woman, she took his breath away. She pulled the black fitted gloves off and uncovered long graceful fingers, no rings. Next she slowly lowered the zipper to expose a spotted fawn. A newborn, by the size of the tiny thing.

He sighed. She should have known better. "Nikki, you never pick up babies. Its mother will be back looking for it."

She brought her eyes up and shook her head. "I know that. The doe was there, but she was… Well, I'm not…I couldn't leave a baby there, alone."

Lifting his hat, he pushed his hair back. "No. Let me take her to the shed. The biggest risk at this point is shock. I'll put her in the covered area with my horse."

For a moment her arms tightened. "Will she be safe? She's too little to be alone." There was a moment while she gazed at the fawn. He wanted to hug her and reassure her that the baby would be fine. He suspected this tough woman hid a soft heart.

"Actually the moms leave them alone all the time, but hidden. There are some wooden crates she can hide in, and we can keep your jacket on her. She seems to like you."

Nikki's summer-blue eyes narrowed as if she was deciding if she could trust him. He waited.

With a nod, she gathered up the sleeping fawn and handed her up to him. The long fragile legs kicked out as they transferred her to Adrian's arms. Once he had her close to his chest, she looked up at him with huge dark eyes.

Mia was going to flip. His daughter was obsessed with furry babies, and this was about the sweetest one he could imagine. "The ranch has the supplies and facilities to care for her. We've raised a few other wild animals along with some calves and goats."

"Sounds like you're a regular Noah."

"No, just a cowboy. I'll be right back."

After getting the little one tucked away and checking on Zeta, he headed back to Nikki. Stuffing away the uncomfortable feelings she created, he took the steps in one leap. He didn't need to start a new relationship, and he doubted Nikki would be interested anyway.

Back in high school, she had been three

grades ahead of him and his brother. So far out of his league he doubted she even knew he existed. He paused at the edge of the porch and looked at her. She had known he wasn't his twin, George. Most people still confused them, but she knew.

She rubbed her face. "Thank you for helping. I'm so embarrassed. I can't believe I managed to get my bike snarled with this stupid brace." Her muscles bunched as she pulled at the twisted metal.

He went to his knee and placed his hand over hers. "Easy. I think you're making it worse."

She leaned her head back and sighed. "Did she settle in?"

"She went right back to sleep, snuggled in your jacket."

"Thank you for helping. Being impaired always frustrates me. I'm not patient on a good day, and this is not anywhere close to a good day. Right now I want to rip my leg off I'm so mad at it."

"You joined the navy, right? Is that where you got your injury?" Silence hung between them as he worked with the tangle of metal. If he had a flathead, maybe he could create a wedge. "Are there tools in the cabin?"

She tried to push herself up.

"No, stay here. I'll check." The cabin was a

bit bigger than it looked from the outside. After going through a few cabinets, he found the utility closet. Inside was an old red toolbox and a worn well-read Bible. *Vanessa Cortez-Bergmann* was printed in gold letters at the bottom. He set it on the table. Nikki might want her mother's Bible.

On the porch, he found her struggling with her brace. "So is it your injury that brought you home after all these years?" He went to work on the chaos of chain and brace.

"You have a lot of questions."

The rain eased a bit, as the thunder rumbled off in the distance. He glanced up at her and found her eyes closed. She seemed to be counting her breaths. What would she say if he told her she had been his first crush in school? When not going to her games, he'd hang out at her family's hardware store just to get a chance to see her or hear her voice. George's teasing had been relentless.

He had more questions, but if she didn't want to talk, he could handle the silence.

She sighed as he moved his focus back to untangling the chain from her brace. The shredded spandex material and mud that covered her knee proved she'd lost the battle between her bike and the rocky hillside.

"I'm out of the navy. I'm an adventure guide

in the Grand Canyon. I'm good at my job, so that's not how I got injured. I need six more weeks of physical therapy before they will even consider releasing me back to work." She rubbed the bridge of her nose, as if telling him that much had drained her.

"Home is a good place to recover. Family can take care of you like no other." He didn't make eye contact, hoping to keep her talking. "Are you staying?"

"I've already missed a couple months of work. I was in the middle of buying my own outfitter company when I had the accident and my roommate decided there were more opportunities elsewhere. If I can get the new doctor to release me sooner, I can be back faster, plus I'm saving money instead of spending. Is that enough information?"

Looking up from his work, he winked at her. "In the last ten years, I haven't been past San Antonio. Sounds like you've had an adventure." And she wanted to get back to it. She had plans to leave. He didn't even know her anymore, so he didn't understand his disappointment.

"I thought bull riders did a lot of traveling. Last I heard, you were on the road for some big purses and the next big thing to hit the PBR."

"I don't ride bulls anymore."

The edge of the brace popped, and she sucked

in her breath. Her hands fisted on the edge of the bench.

"Sorry." He gave her a fast glance.

"It's okay, just surprised me."

Fresh blood bubbled from the wound. Pulling a bandanna out of his pocket, he applied pressure. "Here, hold this. I think I almost have it." He stood and took off his duster. Throwing it over a nearby rocking chair, he went back to work. "So riding your bike off-trail in the rain is part of your therapy?"

"I figured it wouldn't be much different than the stationary bike they have me on in the office."

He laughed. He shook his head as he slipped the last chain from under the metal hinge on her brace. "You might have gone backward in your recovery. The chain did a number on your skin, and the knee looks discolored and swollen. You need to elevate and put ice on it."

Biting hard on her lip, she tilted her head back, eyes squeezed shut. Each breath was deep and hard.

He wanted to cover her free hand and stop it from rubbing her thigh red. He had never seen anyone work so hard not to cry. "Nikki, it's going to be okay."

"I can't take this anymore. I have to get better. I need to get back to work."

"Rushing it will only make the recovery longer." A gust of wind pushed rain onto the porch. "Let's get inside and clean all this mud off. Last thing you want is an infection."

Do not cry. Only the weak cried. She was not weak. The last thing she wanted was Adrian seeing her pathetic self-pity, or anyone, for that matter. Weakness gave people the impression they could use you.

Standing, Nikki tried to put weight on her bad leg, but sharp pain shot up her spine, threatening to bring her to her knees. Swallowing down a scream, she instinctively reached out to Adrian for support.

What she really wanted was to be whole again, independent and strong. She'd get her life back.

She had to. Being in Clear Water was too painful, and it brought secrets too close to the surface.

Twelve years separated her from the past. She had made the mistake thinking she was over it. It was easier to forget when you weren't surrounded by reminders.

Allowing Adrian to help settle her into one of the ladder-back chairs, she traced the patterns in the wood her grandpa had carved. When she saw her mother's study Bible, she stopped breathing. "How did that get here?"

"What? Oh, the Bible. I found it tucked away when I was looking for—"

"Put it back." She closed her eyes. "Please."

"Sure. Sorry. I didn't mean to—"

"I just don't wanna see it." A burn started at her arm. An angry red scratch showed through her fitted shirt. The sleeve of her favorite workout top had a rip running all the way up to the shoulder.

Adrian pulled another chair up close for her useless leg and gently pulled her favorite running shoe off her foot. The timeworn sofa would have been more comfortable, but no telling what critters had moved in under the old cushions or what they might have left behind. The years of dust alone would smother her if she plopped down on the blue plaid fabric.

Images of her and her twin sisters curled up around their mother as she read from her Bible bubbled to the surface. Nikki used to rush to answer the questions at the end of each story. The twins were one year younger than her, but she had wanted to prove she was smarter and better at everything.

Looking back, she was sure it had to do with all the attention they got. Beautiful twin girls did not go unnoticed, but the plain big sister did.

It wasn't their fault.

She never felt that competition with their youngest sister, Samantha. She'd been more of a mother to her. Sammi was the only good thing their stepmother had given their family. Sheila's leaving had been the other good thing, but that happened after she herself had left.

Nikki took in a deep breath. She had no right to judge. Her family needed her, but she'd been too much of a coward to face the consequences of her own mistakes and abandoned everyone that counted on her. She turned away from the living room and closed her eyes.

She couldn't remember the last time she felt smart or accomplished.

Her gaze went back to the river stone fireplace, to the past. It was cold and empty now, not crackling with a warm blaze like her memory. She could see her father sitting on the recliner, telling her to give her sisters a chance.

Remembering the twins when they were little had a tendency to soften her heart. Soft hearts broke easily.

The image needed to leave her head. She didn't have time for regrets or grief. They weren't real anyway. Just pictures she stared at when she was little so she wouldn't forget the way her mom looked.

Her mom was gone, and the twins were

women now. Danica had her own twin daughters. Even little Sammi, who had barely been in school when she left, was now in her twenties and helping run the lumberyard.

Eyes closed, she focused on her body and took deep breaths, pulling in all wayward thoughts. She rotated her foot to evaluate the pain of the injury. Hopefully it wasn't anything that damaged her recovery. A cold chill climbed up her spine. The last thing she needed was another surgery. Adrian had left. His warm touch no longer working on her knee.

The sputtering of water forcing air through old rusted pipes brought her attention back to the present.

Adrian held a bowl at the sink. "After tending that cut, we'll get your knee washed up. Then I'll try and get the mud out of your hair. You must have taken some fall. Was it after or before the rescue?" His shoulders bunched and moved as he rinsed out the bowl and filled it with water. She'd been impressed by the way he snapped the chain and took charge. He might not be riding bulls any longer, but he was still a man of action. He turned. "Do you know if there are any blankets we can trust?"

The rain hit the tin roof. Talking took energy and focus she didn't have right now. "I haven't been here since I was eight."

"That's a shame. It's a great place. There's always someone trying to buy it from your dad or lease it, but rumor has it he won't even talk about it."

"The twins and I actually own the ranch. It's been in my mom's family for five generations and Dad didn't want any problems with Sheila, so he made sure to put it in our names." One of the many things that had made Sheila mad.

He pulled another chair up next to her and carefully wiped at her arm. "That turned out to be a smart idea. This seems like a perfect place for you. One of the highest cliffs in the county is on the far corner of your property. There are rumors of caves, and you have one of the best parts of the river running right through it. It's too rough and small to really run cattle, but you could have your own private adventure park."

"One problem. I'm leaving Clear Water as soon as possible."

"I used to have that goal." He shrugged and winked. "But God had other plans for me, better plans."

She tried to stop him by placing her hand over his. Despite the cold, his skin warmed hers. His fingers were long and surprisingly graceful. The calluses kept them from looking pampered. "Working man hands" was what her dad called them. "You don't have to do that."

"No, but I'm not going anywhere, and it's much more efficient for me to take care of it." He scooted the chair down and removed the brace. "So what did you name your new baby?"

For a second her gut twisted, and she wondered how he knew. *The deer.* He was talking about the fawn. "I thought men talked less than women." She certainly didn't want to talk about babies.

"Now there you go, stereotyping me." He grinned at her.

She almost laughed. When was the last time a man teased her? He might actually be flirting with her, and it was nice. He pressed on the bottom of her knee.

Her jaw locked, and she took a sharp breath in through her nose. She would not cry out. Gaze on the ceiling, she avoided looking at her injury. If she needed another surgery to repair the damage her run at freedom caused, she might actually cry. She never cried. She was tough. It was just mind over matter.

Adrian used the warm cloth to wipe the mud away. His touch surprisingly gentle. He and his twin brother had been a few grades behind her. Everyone joked that her sisters, identical twins, should date the identical twin boys. She remembered him being charming and a favorite with teachers and students. Known as the wild twin, he was the next big thing in the bull-riding world.

At a young age, he had already won two high school state titles and everyone knew when he turned eighteen he would take the PBR by storm.

"How did you go from superstar bull rider to a cowhand for Childress?"

"I haven't been on a bull since I was seventeen. God had better things in store for me."

"What happened? From what I remember, you were a natural. I saw you ride several times. Once, we drove down to San Antonio to watch you." The blood rushed at the memory of watching him ride, one hand in the air as the massive bundle of muscles, horns and hooves went into a spin. "It was amazing. The bull was huge and mean. Even the way you jumped off stuck in my brain. I think you were sixteen. Why did you stop? Were you hurt?"

He looked at her face. The gold flecks in his dark eyes flashed, making him look younger. "You drove to San Antonio to watch me ride?"

She nodded. "A group of us."

With a grin, he went back to work on her leg. He gave a half laugh. "Being hurt is part of the game. What stopped me from riding was my daughter."

"What? You said you stopped at seventeen." There was no way she had heard him right.

He sighed and finally looked up from working on her knee. "Not my finest moment, but I can't regret it. I'm surprised you hadn't heard the gossip. I'm pretty sure the whole Southwest knew about my fall from grace. I was the example worried mamas used to warn their kids that might stray." He broke eye contact and went back to her injury. "Mia was born the end of my junior year. My mom said if I was serious about raising my daughter she'd help me, but I had to leave the rodeo."

Maybe if her mom had been alive, things would have been different for her own senior year. She thought back to the girls at their school. "Is her mother a local or did you meet her at a show?"

"Do you remember Charlotte Walker?"

"Yeah. She was new in town, and…anyway. So you gave up your bull riding to get married and raise a family?"

A noise that might be described as a laugh sounded from his throat, but it lacked any humor. "No. Never got married. Being a mother was not in Charlotte's plans. She wanted to give Mia up for adoption. She left us and went on with her life as if Mia never happened."

Nikki fought the instinct to defend the teen

mother, but she knew it wasn't Charlotte she was protecting. It was her own ugly past. She never, ever thought about the son she'd walked away from. She couldn't.

Tommy hadn't been willing to even acknowledge her in public. She bit the inside of her cheek hard and kept her gaze trained on Adrian's hands. She couldn't risk looking at him.

Twisting the cloth, he dunked it back in the water. "But it worked out fine. I don't have any regrets when it comes to my daughter."

He went on as if he hadn't taken her to the darkest places she worked so hard to avoid and keep buried.

"Mom always hated that I rode bulls. I think she was secretly happy to have that leverage over me. I got a job and finished high school."

Nikki didn't know what to say. "Wow." Okay, that was lame. "You went to work for Dub Childress?"

"I only started working horses for him part-time about a couple of years ago. I thought Mia was old enough for me to be back in the arena. Not bulls, but with horses. I really missed that part. I volunteer with the youth rodeo and horse club." A throaty laugh made her nerve endings tingle. "Can you believe I'm the 4-H dad? Life takes us to strange and wonderful places we never even knew we wanted. I don't really miss the bulls."

She imagined he missed it more than he would ever admit. Did he say it to remind himself the way she had to remind herself she was tough and better off alone? After a few minutes of silence, he looked back up at her and grinned.

"George and I have a construction company. We started doing odd jobs, but found we're really good at restoring old homes. Next week we might actually start a job for your dad. Your sisters wanted to remodel the upstairs of the hardware store for some time now." He stood. "But you probably knew that already. Everyone has different ideas, and your dad always said no to the project. He asked us to come by Monday and give him an estimate. He has a firm budget, so we aren't sure what we'll be able to do." Taking the bowl to the sink, he dumped the dirty water and refilled it.

"No, I didn't."

He turned and leaned against the counter with his hands braced on the edge. He reminded her of one of her grandmother's odd sayings. *That man is a tall drink of water.* She'd never understood what it meant until now.

He turned back to the sink and rinsed the cloth. Finished, he started walking to her, an easygoing smile marking long dimples on his cheeks. Her pulse kicked up a notch. "I'm fine. Everything's clean. You can go."

Thunder and lightning gave her sentence an exclamation mark.

"Are you kicking me out into the storm?"

She didn't want to feel better because of his smile or that he was nice to her. If he knew the truth, it would all change. "The rain should let up soon. Why were you on the ranch anyway? My father gets nasty about people trespassing. At least he used to."

"Still does. Riding the fence, I found a section down. The storm hit while I was checking to see if any of our cattle had wandered over to your land."

He walked toward her and she narrowed her eyes. What was he going to do now? Whenever anyone was this nice to her, they wanted something. "You could wait on the porch or check on your horse. What about the fawn? Should we make sure she's all right?"

"You have twigs and mud tangled in your hair. Let me help you at least get the pieces of tree out of your scalp. What happened out there anyway?"

"What do you know about hair?" She knew she sounded snarky, but the thought of him coming closer set her nerves on edge.

He didn't slow down. "I'm a single dad of a

ten-year-old girl. You'd be amazed how much I know about hair."

Standing behind her, Adrian started pulling out random debris that she had collected on her downhill slide. Soft tugs on her scalp actually soothed her. So he was going to ignore her hints to leave. She closed her eyes. "You're really good at this."

"A perk of having an active ten-year-old daughter. I know how to untangle the biggest mess without pulling out any hair." He moved to the other side and his fingers started at the base of her neck. "Mia has long curly hair that's incredibly thick. I try to keep it braided or at least in a rubber band. One time while we were shearing my dad's angoras, I found her in the middle of a pen full of mama goats and their kids. They had nibbled her hair all the way up to her shoulders."

Even the steady rhythm of his voice lured her to relax and trust him. "Was she upset?"

"No. She's a great kid. She laughed and said she needed a haircut anyway." His fingers ran through her strands one more time. "Sorry, I tend to talk about her too much." Rich sounds of laughter danced across the forgotten family retreat. "She gets a little put out with me, but that's my job, right? So how are we going to get you home? I don't think you're in any shape to ride a horse. Do you have a phone? Mine's dead, and I don't see a landline here. I'm sure your dad's worried."

"I think my dad stopped worrying about me a long time ago."

"Dads never stop worrying. My dad still tells me what I should be doing, how to do it and what I'm doing wrong. Can't imagine giving up that card for Mia either."

Giving him a light shrug, she leaned her head back and closed her eyes. So Adrian was the perfect father. Great, just what she needed—another reminder of all the ways she had messed up her life. *Let me count the ways.* "I'll just wait until the storm passes. Then I'll walk back to town."

"That's about ten miles from here. I can't believe you biked this far on that knee. Not gonna happen, and I'm not leaving you here alone. So do you have a phone on you?"

"You have to push through the pain if you're going to make any gains." She crossed her arms.

He mirrored her and leaned to the side, shifting his weight to his left leg. He didn't say another word, just stared at her, waiting for an answer.

"You're not giving up, are you?" She had to respect his quiet tenacity.

"Nope."

"Fine. I didn't bring one because I didn't want anyone to find me, but there should be an old landline in the office behind the stairs. And yes, I might have overdone it on the knee." With the same swagger he had as a bull rider, Adrian cut across the room. Back in school, even the older girls would sigh when he walked past in his Wranglers.

Palms pressed against her face, she blocked the sight. She had no business noticing his swagger. Eye candy was not her thing. It just got a girl in trouble.

Back in high school, Tommy had been all smiles and charm wrapped up in a good-looking package. She wanted to be loved so bad she believed his lies. Then in Arizona, sweet eye-candy Mike captivated her and convinced her he was ready to take on an adventure as long as she was there. Look where that got her. Both men almost destroyed her.

She had one goal. Get healthy and get back to the Grand Canyon. Well, that was two, but the one thing she knew for sure: Adrian De La Cruz needed to stay out of her head. She didn't worry about her heart. It was already gone.

Chapter Two

Adrian tossed the trashed bike into the back of Mr. Bergmann's truck. The rain had moved east and now humidity sat heavy on his shoulders as he stood at the driver's door. "Mr. Bergmann, I'll get the fence repaired before the weekend is out."

"Appreciate it, Adrian. And thanks for helping Nicole." He cut a glance to his daughter. "She shouldn't have even been out here. It's too hazardous, and with her bashed-up knee she could have gotten herself killed. This place is dangerous." With the sigh of a frustrated father, he looked back at Adrian. "I thank God you were out here."

Arms crossed over her chest, she rolled her eyes. "I can take care of myself. No one had to save me, Daddy." She sighed and leaned forward. "Adrian, thank you. I'm grateful you were here. I'm just… Let me know if there is anything I need to do for the fawn."

He understood her frustration. Needing help was never a fun place to be in when you were used to taking care of yourself. "No worries—we've got her. You can visit anytime you like. Consider it an open adoption." He chuckled. "Glad I was here. Hope there's not too much damage to your knee."

The diesel engine roared to life. Bergmann tipped his Montana Brand tools baseball cap. "I'll see you at the store Monday if not before."

Adrian gave a slap to the door and stepped back. He waited for them to disappear around the curve before heading to the shed. With a hind leg cocked, Zeta looked to be sound asleep. "Hey, wake up, lazy. We've got a fence to fix." After calling Nikki's dad, he had called George to let him know he'd be late to dinner.

Ears forward, she raised her head. "Yeah, yeah, yeah. You were just waiting on me." After checking the gear, he picked up the fawn and tucked her inside his duster, close to him. "We have a guest, so mind your manners." He let the horse smell the baby deer then patted her withers before swinging up into the saddle. With a nudge of his knees, they started down the dirt road at a more leisurely pace than a few hours ago.

At the downed fence, he saw a Childress work truck with the cutting-horse logo on the side. His brother, George, pulled fencing from the back. Mia started jumping and waving.

She was trying to jump, anyway. She looked a bit awkward with the new brace. He'd be so happy when he didn't have to see a brace again. Mia's gear looked twice as long as Nikki's. She never did tell him what kind of injury she suffered.

"Mia, careful. We just got your cast off. Where're your crutches?" Dismounting, he dropped the reins to the ground. "You shouldn't have brought her out here. She's going to end up back in the wheelchair."

"Hey, you were the one who left her at school without calling, so don't lecture me, little brother. Anyway, I remember someone with a busted ankle refusing to use his crutches." George and Mia moved to the fence. She carried the fence ties as she limped next to his twin. "Then you cut the thing off so you wouldn't miss another ride. She'll be fine, Papa Bear."

Adrian popped his jaw. He was not in the mood for his brother's ribbing. He moved to the back seat of the Silverado 2500 and used a blanket to wrap the sleeping fawn. He'd surprise Mia with it on the way back to the ranch.

"My injury was different. She's a ten-year-old girl and could get hurt again."

"You need to relax. What has you so uptight? What are you doing in the truck?"

"Nothing. And you're not a father, so you don't get it."

George stopped what he was doing and straightened. "I can't believe you said that to me. Are you looking for a fight? Because I can give you one right here and leave you in the mud, little brother."

Mia rolled her eyes. "*Tío* George, it's okay. He just freaks out easily since I fell off the horse. It all worked out. And, Daddy, if I sit at home any longer I'll scream. Please don't get mad at *Tío*."

"You didn't just fall off your horse. You were dragged across an arena."

George narrowed his eyes and scrutinized his twin. Adrian glared back for a moment, but quickly turned away, studying the blue sky that had been heavy and threatening an hour ago. If anyone could see his discomfort over seeing Nikki again, it would be his twin. "Weather changes fast around here."

"Sure." George started unrolling the wire. "Hold this, *mija*. Changing the subject won't work. When you called you said the oldest Bergmann sister was hurt. Didn't know she was back in town. Still as stunning as when she was in school?"

Adrian scowled at his brother then back to his daughter. Was his brother that dense to talk about women in front of Mia? He followed the glare with a shrug. "I don't know what you're talking about. She was hurt, and I helped her. She's in a brace too, and was doing stuff she shouldn't have been doing." He took the coiled wire fencing from Mia. "Go put the tailgate down and sit with the dogs. The ground is too wet and uneven for your injured leg."

"Daddy! *Tío* said I could help."

"Go or I'll have your *tío* take you home."

With a heavy sigh, she limped back to the truck. Beast and Belle, George's blue heelers, got excited and sat next to her. Those were the kind of names you got when a six-year-old girl named your dogs. She hugged the pair and let them lick her. He sighed.

Now she'd probably name any new dogs after some boy-band crush. She was growing up too fast, and there was nothing he could do to stop the changes.

He checked his watch. Sitting still was hard for Mia. Who was he kidding? He'd go crazy not being able to work. He knew she thought he was too stern, so did his brother, but he couldn't deal with her being hurt again. "How about I take you to the store when we finish? You can get a couple of new coloring books and markers. I need to pick up some groceries anyways."

Her face lit up. "Thank you, Daddy!"

When she smiled, he automatically felt guilty for being upset with her. Seeing Nikki all grown up, but hurt and refusing help, had put him in a bad mood.

Tuesday, they had the first physical-therapy session with the new brace. The therapist only came to Clear Water twice a week. Nikki would probably be there.

He sighed and pulled the wire tight. The high school girl he obsessed over no longer existed. Life had taken them in different directions. She took on the world, and he was happy living within the borders of Clear Water, raising his daughter.

"Nikki, don't be stubborn. I can cancel my appointment and go to The Mercantile for you." Her father kept looking straight ahead. He hated conflict and would avoid it at all cost.

She pushed the door open. "I just need a few things. I can walk over to the hardware store when I'm finished. I need to work out the kinks."

The muscle in his jaw popped. "It's the walking part I'm worried about." The wrinkles at the edges of his eyes and the gray in his hair marked the time she had been away. If she allowed herself to put a number to the years, she might start crying…and never stop. So many regrets that couldn't be undone.

"I've got this, Daddy. I'm used to being on my own."

"You are not alone. You've never been alone. We've been here the whole time, waiting. I never asked you to leave. I…" He took a deep breath. "I understood why you left, but once your stepmother was gone, why didn't you come back? The door was always opened for you."

"Sheila was never any kind of mother, step or otherwise." This was exactly the reason she never came home. Adjusting her ponytail, Nikki pulled it tight. "I know I would be welcomed home. I just needed to move on from Clear Water." She jerked the handle harder than necessary and stepped out onto the golf-ball-sized gravel. "If you don't leave now you'll be late, and a Bergmann is never late. Love you."

As she tried to walk away with a straight spine, the uneven concrete steps slowed her down. She paused on the top one. She had never been good at being truthful with herself.

It was not the four lopsided steps that stopped her, but the thought of going in the store and seeing people she hadn't seen in years. Maybe she should have let her dad go for her so she could keep hiding in the house.

A couple more steps and she forced herself to open the glass door. The tiny bell rang and the few people in the store turned and looked at her before going back to their business, everyone except Victoria Lawson. Well, Miller since she married Tommy. Barbed wire tightened around her spine.

Vickie was one of the people she didn't want to see. The one person she never dreamed would be working in a small-town grocery store. The one person she owed the biggest apology to. She didn't think Vickie even knew. Maybe she had been wrong keeping silent. At the time, she thought telling everyone would just cause more hurt all around.

The former head cheerleader and class president came around the counter and hugged her. "Nikki Bergmann, it's great seeing you. Danica told me you were in town. Welcome back." In high school, she'd been the perfect girl dating the perfect quarterback. There was a petty, dark part of Nikki that was disappointed her secret high school rival was still as beautiful, maybe even more so. Last she heard, Vickie and Tommy were at Baylor University together and had a son a year after she had her... *Stop it, Nikki!*

Shifting from one foot to the other, she tried to come up with something polite to say. People made small talk. It was normal. *Be normal.*

She hated chitchat. Forcing a smile, she returned Vickie's hug then stepped back. "Thank you. So you and Tommy moved back to Clear Water?"

"Where have you been? I can't believe your sisters didn't tell you. I moved back to Clear Water without Tommy. We're divorced and he's, well... He's not around."

For a moment, her brain shut down. Not a single neuron fired. "Oh, I...I'm sorry."

Vickie laughed. "Don't be. Jake Torres and I are married now. Coming back was the best thing that ever happened to me. Maybe God has something great in store for you too." She smiled, a real smile, not the smirk she used back in high school. "I finally got smart. So what brought you in today?" She glanced down at Nikki's leg. "Anything I can get for you?"

"I just need a cart." She tried smiling again, but it felt tight. Between the pain traveling from her leg to her spine, and the emotions of guilt, her lungs burned from the lack of air. Vickie was married to Jake, not Tommy. All the horrible feelings when she was a teenager started crowding out the person she worked hard to become while she was away from Texas. Another reason she didn't want to ever step foot in Clear Water again.

The wood floors under her feet had to be over a hundred years old. How many people had walked through here, taking care of their families? People that didn't run away. She needed painkillers. She needed them over an hour ago.

Vickie brought a small wobbly wheeled shopping cart over to her. Leaning into it, Nikki almost cried from the relief of taking pressure off her leg.

Stomping off from her dad had been a bad choice. Her whole leg throbbed, and it was her own fault. *Yeah, that's her, a living, breathing, limping example of pride cometh before the fall.*

The shopping cart pulled to the left again. She growled and yanked it back. Great, she had a lame basket too.

"Nikki?"

She dropped her head before plastering a smile on her face and turning to Adrian. "If I didn't know better, I'd think you were stalking me."

"Maybe you do know better, and you're onto me." His heart-melting smile was highlighted by a wink.

She glared at him. Did she look like the kind that invited flirting? Most of the men in her life didn't even try.

He dared to lean in closer and grinned. "Do you need help? What are you getting?"

"I'm just getting some painkillers, almond milk and orange juice. But I've got it."

"Daddy! Look, they have a new horse book. Can I get it too?" A beautiful girl of about ten hobbled over on crutches, her long dark hair trying to crawl out of a French braid.

Nikki froze. Her gut twisted. Adrian's daughter.

"Mia, this is Nikki Bergmann. She's the long-lost oldest Bergmann sister. We went to school together. Nikki, my daughter, Mia."

"Oh, you saved Swift. She's so sweet. Thank you for giving her to my dad. I promise to take good care of her and you can come see her anytime. So you went to school with my dad. Did you know my mom?"

Adrian cut his daughter a glare. "Mia."

"Sorry. Daddy says you have a brace too." The girl looked at her leg in confusion. "Did they let you take it off?"

She watched Adrian walk the short distance to the cooler at the end of the aisle. He was a man now with a man's filled-out frame, but he still had the I-own-the-world swagger that seemed to be in all bull riders. It was hard to believe he gave it up for his daughter. She glanced at Mia. Did he have regrets? Obviously Charlotte, Mia's mother, was a banned subject.

The silence didn't deter the young girl. "I just got my cast off, and Tuesday I have my first day in full therapy. I have a rod and screws holding my leg together. Are you in physical therapy?"

She was as talkative as her dad. Nikki blinked a few times to clear her thoughts. "I'll be there at sixteen hundred hours."

Adrian tossed a bottle of orange juice and a carton of unsweetened almond milk in her cart as he laughed. "For us civilians, we need to translate." He rolled his eyes up as he counted on his fingers. He looked back at them with a grin. "Four o'clock, right?"

The girl's face lit up. "Yay! We can be workout buddies. Daddy said you're an adventure guide in the Grand Canyon and you were in the navy. That sounds really cool. I broke my leg in three places being drug by a horse in the arena. I hit my head, so I don't remember any of it, but Daddy saw everything." The same gold flecks her father had now flashed in her young eyes.

"Mia." Adrian looked as if he had lost some color to his dark skin and his eyebrows had a deep crease between them. He did not share Mia's excitement over the story of her accident.

Leaning closer to her, Mia whispered, "Daddy's having a harder time dealing with my injury than I am."

"Sorry, she thinks everyone wants to hear her life story."

"Wonder who she got that from?" She winked at Adrian. He actually blushed. Without thought, laughter—good honest laughter—bubbled forth. It surprised her at first. She didn't laugh often—not much to laugh about.

Mia didn't seem to notice her dad's discomfort. "Did you fall while climbing cliffs, or smash against a rock in the white-water rapids? I've seen shows about it."

"No, just a boring car wreck." She smiled at Mia. "I busted my ACL and damaged my meniscus."

"Oh no. Is everyone okay?" Her small hand went to her chest.

"Yeah. I got the worst of it. A guy on his cell phone T-boned us. As the passenger, I took the main hit." That wasn't the only hit she took that day. She shifted her weight, trying to take the pressure off her hurt knee.

"Why aren't you wearing a brace?" The concerned look on Mia's face mirrored Adrian's. The child undeniably had more of her dad in her than her mom. All she remembered of Charlotte was the girl liked wearing black and never smiled—not at her, anyway. She couldn't picture Adrian being with a girl like that.

Since he apparently didn't have a cart, Adrian just threw some fresh carrots, corn on the cob and spinach in hers. He also had a giant supply of painkillers and a bottle of water. "She was doing stuff she shouldn't be doing and now she's in pain and might have hurt her knee all over again. We had to cut her brace off so she could walk." He opened the painkillers and held three gel tablets out to her. "Why don't you take a few of these now. You look as if you won't be standing much longer."

"I'm fine." She wanted to refuse the meds he offered her, but she knew he was right. She had waited too long and now the pain was overwhelming. Without the cart she wouldn't be standing. She took them from his hand and slammed them back without the water he offered. "Thanks."

With a gentle nudge, he turned her cart to the front of the old store. "Let's get you checked out and drive you home. You need to elevate and ice that knee. No more walking."

Mia sighed. "Sorry he's so bossy. He says that all the time to me. Daddy thinks ice cures everything. *Tío* says it's from his bull-riding days. Ice it, wrap it and get back in the saddle." The little girl dropped her voice to mimic her father.

"Except you will not be getting back in the saddle—not on a barrel racer, anyway."

The smaller version of Adrian crossed her arms and tightened her mouth, but she didn't say anything. There was trouble in paradise.

"Hey, Nikki." George came from the back, carrying something wrapped in white butcher paper.

The brothers still looked a great deal alike, but she never understood how people got them confused. Adrian was leaner and better looking. She always thought so, anyway.

George smiled. "Good to see you. How's the knee?" They did have the same smile, but George's didn't make her feel weak.

"She's in pain and needs to get off her feet. We're checking out then taking her home." Adrian moved her cart slowly to the checkout. Another difference: George wasn't as bossy as his twin.

"Great, you're joining us for dinner. Good thing I decided to pick up a couple of extra steaks."

Adrian placed the items on the worn laminate counter and smiled at Vickie as she started ringing them up. "Not our house. We're taking her to her home."

"Nikki, you should come over and let us pamper you. My grilled steaks and corn on the cob is famous, and Adrian tosses a mean spin-ach salad."

Vickie chuckled as she put the unhusked corn in a bag. "It's true. No one passes up an opportunity for George's grilling." She picked up the pills and started putting them in the bag too.

"No, those are mine." Reaching for them, Nikki winced as the pain shot through her body. "I'm paying for those."

Adrian's hand balanced her. "Careful. Just put it on my tab." He looked at George. "Get the bags. I'm taking her to the truck."

"Your daughter's right. You're bossy." Biting down on the inside of her cheeks, she let Adrian lead her out the door. As they approached the steps, she wanted to cry. There was no way she was going to make it.

Without warning, her feet left the ground and Adrian had her cradled in his arms like a big giant baby. "I can walk."

"Right. I knew you were going to say that, which is why I didn't bother to ask. I've never seen someone so stubborn about being in pain, and I used to hang out with bull riders. You're much easier to carry without a bike attached to you."

A group of boys walked by, and all the girls giggled.

"Adrian, you finally catch a girlfriend?" one of the boys yelled out.

Another followed up. "He found one that wasn't fast enough." The boys laughed at their own stupid jokes.

Adrian shook his head and gave her a half grin before turning back to the boys. "Seth, make yourself useful and open my back door."

"Yes, sir." The lanky kid ran past them and stood next to the door.

He looked familiar, but she couldn't place him. Adrian eased her into the back seat and turned her so her legs stretched out.

"Seth!" The kid was already back on the sidewalk when Adrian yelled at him. "I forgot to tell your mom that Dr. Rankin had to reschedule. Next month the horse-club meeting needs to be moved to the seventeenth. Go ask your mom to send an email out to all the members. She's just inside."

"Yes, sir." The kid smiled.

Her throat went dry as a face from her past flashed across her mind. "Was that Tommy and Vickie's son?"

He pulled the seat belt around so she could buckle it. "Yep. He's about twelve. It's been a bit rough on him, but he's a good kid."

"Rough? Because of the divorce? Seth looks like his father."

"Yeah, he does. The divorce was bad enough, but then… Tommy's in jail."

"Tommy Miller?" She blinked. The world turned upside down. He had been the golden boy. Everyone loved him. She had loved him, until he used her and… "Why?"

"Domestic violence. The worst part was Seth was the one to call 911 and had to step between his father and Vickie. Tommy threatened her with a gun." He closed the door.

Numb. Her brain was numb.

Mia opened the other passenger door and crawled up into the bench seat. "Are you going to eat with us?"

"No, Mia. She needs to go home."

Nikki looked up at Adrian. Their eyes met in the mirror. "Please." She wanted to say more, but if she uttered another word she would start to cry.

One quick nod, and he turned the key. George got in the front and handed her a small bag. "Sure you don't want to join us? We have plenty."

Adrian backed the truck out. "She needs to go home and get some rest. I think her day's been long enough."

Sometimes being bossy was a good thing. Nikki closed her eyes, thankful that Adrian understood on some level that she needed to hide.

At this rate, she shouldn't venture out of her father's house ever again. Not until it was time to leave Clear Water, anyway.

Chapter Three

Hiding in the corner—well, actually a closet—Nikki sat on an odd chair that had been left behind. Her father wanted her to meet with Adrian and George as they did an appraisal of the remodel. She knew he was trying to get her out of the house and involved in the family business. She would have said no, but she was starting to get a little stir-crazy.

Now she regretted the decision to come to the lumberyard. At least George would be here. She just didn't want to spend any more time alone with Adrian.

From the dark cubby, she could see through several open doors to the front area. Built in 1884, parts of the store had seen better days. Some of the interior walls had been torn down sometime in the twenties or thirties to make the front half one big room. Rumor had it they used it for dancing, but she couldn't imagine any-one in her father's family hosting community dances. Eight columns supported the stamped tin ceiling, and a raised platform gave credence to the live music gatherings. The back part of the space had been living quarters.

The ornate door that she remembered always being locked now leaned against the wall. A heavy carved chair with a strange back elevated above the others in a sea of forgotten chairs. The different styles stood as evidence of each decade that marched through the rooms. It looked as if generations of Bergmanns never threw any-thing away.

Over the years, her father stood firm that the cost to repair the upstairs of the historic build-ing had been out of financial reach. Money needed to be spent wisely on the areas where customers traveled. Which meant the above and below were left untouched. The basement was used as storage for the business, but the upper floor looked like a graveyard of the forgotten.

Footsteps on the narrow staircase to her left stopped her thoughts. One pair of boots slowly moved closer to her. Only one?

Please, let it be George. He didn't ask her questions or make her uncomfortable.

The man on the stairs came into view. He

had his back to her. Her stomach dropped with a heavy thud. It was Adrian.

Worn fitted Levi's jeans, boots and a blue button-up shirt tucked neatly had him looking all business with a pair of work gloves in his back pocket. The silver Stetson was not the same one he'd worn when he hauled her out of the rain.

He wasn't much taller than she remembered. But he had filled out. In a very nice way. Too nice for her comfort.

Hands on his hips, he arched back and studied the ceiling. He moved through the doors to the front of the room and stopped at one of the large ten-foot windows.

She had a perfect view as he gently ran his fingers along the wood trim then dropped to the floor and thoughtfully traced the baseboards.

He muttered some words she couldn't hear then turned his attention to the broken laminate tiles in the floor. Slowly, he pried one of the squares up and touched the flooring he found underneath. He caressed the building as if comforting and reassuring hurt feelings.

Standing, he turned her way. His eyes went wide for a second, and then he smiled at her. "Well, Ms. Bergmann, what a pleasure to find you hiding up here." In a few steps, he stood in front of her. The morning sun flooded through the windows behind him. The light made it hard to see the details of his face.

Why did she feel guilty for watching him? "I'm not hiding. Daddy asked me to meet you and George here." Standing over her, he seemed taller than six foot. Using the arm of the chair, she got herself to her feet. "He wanted to make sure you didn't get any crazy ideas of making a grand statement with the remodel. He's still not sure he wants to waste the money on this part of the building." She looked to the back stairway. Maybe George got stopped downstairs by one of her sisters. "Where's your partner?"

"My partner needed to finish up another job and sent me. My specialty is uncovering the beauty in old buildings. I can keep it as simple or as complicated as you want it."

"Simple. I… We…I mean, he, my father, wants to keep it simple."

"What about your sisters? They gave me a long list of ideas, and every time they saw me they added more." He crossed his arms over his chest, and his shirt stretched across lean hard muscles. She looked toward the door, not wanting to remember how comforting it felt to be held by those arms. He had just been helping someone in trouble. He hadn't meant anything by it.

"My sisters are great with ideas, but Daddy's the money man."

He nodded as his eyes scanned the room. "What about you? What part are you playing?"

"Not any. I'm just a temporary guest who plans to move on as soon as I can."

His attention came back to her and he paused until they made eye contact. "That's a shame."

Now, why did her insides have to get all gooey? Ugh, she had the worst taste in men. He was a bull rider. Maybe a retired one, but still, they were all adrenaline junkies and thought they were some kind of gift to the women of the planet. It must have to do with the arrogance of thinking they could ride a two-thousand-pound animal made of muscle. She had enough issues without dating a risk taker, and he had a kid. That made him off-limits.

Stay on topic, Nikki girl. You're here to talk about the building. "So what do you think? Can it be made into usable space at a reasonable price?"

He ran his fingertips along the decorative cuts on the unhinged door. "My guess from the designs cut into the wood is that this door was brought over from Europe, maybe Germany. This is one solid piece of wood, not small pieces glued on. It's beautiful." His gaze cut across the room. "I had no clue there was such a big pulley up here. The wheel is at least eight feet wide. It's amazing."

She could see the appreciation in his eyes.

He waved her to follow him. "Come here."

Without waiting, he moved to a moldy part of the wall that had started to crumble. He took the work gloves from his back pocket. With them on, he carefully lifted a corner of the drywall and pulled. It gave way under the pressure, and he moved back.

With a gleam he looked at her, waiting for her reaction. He acted as if he was sharing a found treasure.

Looking at the exposed stone wall then back at him, she waited.

"This is incredible and a pretty easy fix." He stepped over the new debris and laid his palm on the stone-and-plaster wall. "Come here."

Carefully she stepped around the rubble and touched the wall.

"Do you feel that? That's a building that has provided shelter and a living for over one hundred and thirty years. It's been covered and hidden away." He gazed at the wall, his hand pressing against it as if listening for a heartbeat. He looked at her and smiled. "Do you feel it?"

The cool stone seemed to have a life all its own. "So you want to take the Sheetrock down and expose the stone."

He nodded. "It was probably added in the sixties trying to make the room look more modern. The fifties and sixties did a great deal of damage to these old places."

Their hands were close. Would he tear down her walls and expose the truth she had hidden? He wouldn't be as excited at what he found there. She feared the damage went too deep.

His rich, warm eyes searched her face. Oh no, he looked as if he might kiss her. His breath was warm and had a faint smell of citrus, like he just ate an orange. They now stood less than an inch apart.

She blinked. She didn't move away from him, and that scared her most. She actually leaned in.

"Hello!"

"Hello!" The greeting's echo came from the back stairs as her twin sisters emerged. Each holding a cup of coffee.

In the same motion, Adrian and she turned away from the wall, away from each other, and faced her sisters. She glared at them. "I thought y'all were running the store while Daddy went to Uvalde."

"Oh, Sammi has it under control—"

"She's been asking for more responsibility—"

"And we are so excited about what Adrian is going to do up here—"

"Adrian, can you see this as a quaint teahouse

with mix-matched chairs and sofas? Lots of books and—"

"There are less than four hundred people in Clear Water, and only three like hot tea. Daddy will not go for a tearoom." Rolling her eyes, Danica turned to Adrian. "I think it should be more practical, maybe a dual purpose. A nice place where people can meet, maybe even have small receptions and parties."

Jackie gave an identical eye roll. "That is soooo practical, Dani."

Nikki rubbed her leg. Her head started to throb. Not much changed with her sisters. She should have never agreed to leave the house, to meet with Adrian. The almost kiss was too close for comfort. She took a deep breath and tried to figure out a way to leave.

Adrian lowered his head to hide his grin. He hoped he and his twin didn't sound like this. Maybe it was a sister thing. But he didn't think they would appreciate his humor at their expense.

All three sisters were tall, almost his height, so they had to be at least five-nine. Nikki was the tallest. The twins had long strawberry blond hair, Danica's in a fancy braid down her back with a few strands curled around her face. When she had first dropped out of college and came home to have her twins, everyone tried setting them up, but all he could think about when he was around her was her older sister Nikki.

It wasn't right to think about one sister when having dinner with the other. So they became good friends.

Danica pointed to Nikki. "She gave me another idea. We could expand the business to camping, hunting and outdoor adventure stuff like the business she wanted to buy at the Grand Canyon."

"What? How did I get drawn into this? I'm not staying." Nikki gave her sister a heated glare as she rubbed her leg. They weren't listening to her. "Why would you think that? I still plan on going through with that once I'm completely healed."

"I think it's a perfect plan. With that jerk of a boyfriend causing your injury, and then taking half of your money, you need family around you. It'd take less funding to start your business in Clear Water. Your dreams can happen here and we can help."

Nikki froze. He watched for any movement, but it looked as if she had stopped breathing.

Adrian went to her side and touched her shoulder. He made sure not to stand too close. The smell of ivory soap had never been so dangerous to his sanity. "Where are your crutches? You need to get off your leg."

He knew she had to be hurting when she allowed him to guide her to one of the antique chairs. It didn't take a genius to figure out she hated showing any weakness, and her sister just put her business out there like it was nothing. They probably saw her troubles as a blessing that brought her home.

Family was like that, manipulating a situation to get you to do what they thought was best. All from love, but it still burned for someone as independent as Nikki. All he could do for her was change the topic.

"This chair looks like another antique from Europe. My best guess without research is it's a prayer chair from France. Has it always been here?"

The twins both shrugged.

"There is so much history in this building. Your family history." Adrian stepped past Nikki and went deeper into the space. The morning sun cast the colors of a high stained-glass window across the room. Purples, blues and greens danced on the old plaster-and-stone wall, creating a feeling of peace, like they were surrounded by water. It had not been touched by so-called modern improvements.

Nikki turned her face to the light and closed

her eyes. The reflection from the antique stained glass touched her features with color. He stopped breathing. An irresistible mix of strength and femininity made up the curves of her face. He needed to pull himself together. That kiss had been too close. What had he been thinking?

The twins crowded the door. "What do you think it is?"

Adrian took his eyes off Nikki, and blinked at her sisters a couple of times before realizing they had not been reading his thoughts. "I think it might've been a prayer room."

"A prayer room?" A hushed whisper couldn't hide their curiosity and awe.

"I've never heard such a thing. Why wouldn't Dad—"

"Why is Samantha alone with a line of customers?" Mr. Bergmann's voice caused them all to jump like kids caught stealing cookies.

Jackie had her hand on her chest. "Really, Daddy? Did you have to scare us?"

"It's your guilty conscience, not me. I told y'all to stay away while Adrian was doing the appraisal. I don't want your fancy ideas to interfere with his bid."

"Daddy, there is so much cool family stuff up here. I'm excited about what we'll find." Jackie stepped closer to her father. At six-five, he towered over his daughter. None of them appeared the slightest bit intimidated. He glanced back at Nikki. Boredom stamped her face, but his gut told him it was an act.

"We are not here to dig up old history. Danica, what are you doing here? Mondays you're at the animal sanctuary. You." Mr. Bergmann looked at Jackie. "You should be downstairs helping your little sister. Someone wants more information about those new chalk paints of yours."

"Daddy, this isn't just family history, but even more important information about what was going on in the area and state." Jackie served on every committee in the area that had anything to do with local and Texas history.

"No. If we remodel that's fine, but that's the end of it. It's not becoming a museum for people to stomp around."

Jackie started to say something else, but Danica took her sister's hand. "It's okay. We're here about the room." With her arm around her sister, she smiled at their father. "We've waited so long for this, Daddy, and Nikki doesn't even really care about the room one way or another." She squeezed Jackie around the waist.

"She's right. We're excited about the possibilities of this room. It was our idea to call Adrian. We should be here." Jackie stated her case one more time, but it didn't help.

Mr. Bergmann crossed his arms and glared. "Which is why I'm putting her in charge. She will make sure the job gets done without wasting money on extravagant ideas. Go or I'll send Adrian away and it'll just stay the way it is right now without even hearing a bid."

With matching sighs, the two women headed down the stairs. He turned back to Nikki and Adrian. He was a tall man with thick dark hair that was sprinkled with silver. He didn't look old enough to have four grown daughters, but there was a sadness in the lines of his face that proved his life had not been an easy one. "Nikki, you look like you're in pain. Do you need to go home? Adrian can come back later. We don't have to do this now."

She stood and smiled at him. "No, I'm good. I just forgot how overwhelming the twins can be when they're together."

He snorted. "Welcome to my life. I think it's about time someone got married around here and added a male point of view."

Adrian knew neither of the twins was dating anyone. Danica had mentioned Nikki's boyfriend, but it didn't sound like they were still together or that he was a good guy. He really wanted to know, but couldn't figure out a way to ask without it getting awkward. The silence after that statement made the air heavy.

"Mr. Bergmann, let me show you the walls." Heading back to the exposed stone, he knew the lumberyard owner wouldn't be as moved by sentiment as his daughter.

Nikki followed. "Adrian said this would be one of the easiest parts, and it'd get rid of possible mold."

The tall man nodded. "Yeah, I've been worried about the mold after that last big storm."

"Truthfully, the biggest areas of expense will be the floor and the windows. They'll have to be custom-made, and to restore the trim I would want to use as much of the original wood as possible. To match it can take time. The wood floor might be tricky too. We really won't know how much damage we're dealing with until we remove the tiles. I'll have to get an asbestos report."

Bergmann toed a corner of a floor tile. "Can't we just put some of that laminate wood flooring over the tile?"

Adrian tried to suppress a shudder, at least enough that Mr. Bergmann wouldn't be offended. That was the problem working on someone else's building. To hide the magnificence of the aged beauty was a true injustice to the original craftsmanship. Putting fake wood on the floor and burying the truth even deeper was so wrong.

"Daddy, if we're gonna do this I think we need to do it right. You know the wood under this flooring is irreplaceable. They can't cut that type of wood planks anymore." Her gaze darted to Adrian, and she took a deep breath before turning back to her dad. "I remember you and Mom talking about this. She'd want to see the floors restored. Do you remember that?"

"Yes, but I didn't think you did."

She nodded. "I do. I think we let Adrian strip the old tiles away and at least see what we have underneath. If there is too much damage to the old wood, then we can talk other options." She glanced back at Adrian. "What do you think?"

"I think it's a good place to start. If it's possible, I would love the opportunity to save the original wood."

"Okay, get an estimate to me, and we'll go from there. I'm putting Nikki in charge."

"Me? Why? I'm not staying." She crossed her arms.

"You'll stay until you're healed and this room is repaired. I trust you. Of all my girls, you're the most practical. I've always been able to count on you to get the job done right. The only reason I'm finally going ahead with this is because you're here. You leave, and I call it off." He turned to Adrian. "You have a problem answering to a woman?"

"No, sir."

"Good. Then whenever you're here, she'll be here. She knows construction."

Adrian lifted his hat and ran his fingers through his hair. He had no problem working with women. He'd done it several times before. What he feared was working with Nikki, and not being able to keep it all business.

Chapter Four

Nikki pushed the stationary bike into double time. She had convinced the new coach to let her in early. By the time the therapist arrived, Nikki had already broken a sweat. When she introduced herself as Teresa Ortega, Nikki hoped she concealed her shock. The Teresa Ortega she remembered couldn't be old enough to have this kind of responsibility. She was one of the younger Ortegas of the huge Ortega clan. One thing she did know: all of them were good people.

After a quick assessment and a short lecture about the percentage of reinjuries if she didn't follow protocol, Teresa left her alone to work out.

Wanting to avoid everyone, Nikki had stayed away from town. Adrian said it would take him a week or two to get the quote together, but he needed to take measurements and check out the condition of the existing structure. He would not actually be working, so she convinced her dad she could use the time to rest at home. If she spoke the truth, she would call it by its right name: hiding.

Unfortunately, there were two things she couldn't avoid. The first being her sisters. They thought their mission was to cheer her up and keep her company.

The concept that she wanted to be in a bad mood and did not want to talk to anyone went over their heads. They came anyway, including her sister's six-year-old twin daughters.

Second, she had to come to physical therapy. If she wanted the doctor to sign off on her recovery and get back to her real life, she'd have to focus and get it done.

She made plans to show up early, and if she kept her head down, maybe she could get out before Adrian and his daughter saw her.

Her father might have been the third, but he seemed to be doing a great job of avoiding her. The hurt in his eyes whenever they happened to be in the same room was too heavy for either one of them to handle.

Like the good Bergmanns they were, they didn't talk about something that might turn into a fight. They kept it to themselves. But the burn in her gut told her that strategy was not working.

"Ms. Bergmann!" Mia rushed to her with strong swings of her crutches.

"Mia, careful." Adrian followed at a more leisurely pace, his hand in the front pocket of his jeans. The whites of his eyes had more red than white in them. He looked as if he'd had a rough night. He glanced down at her new shiny knee brace. "How's the knee? Any permanent damage?"

She pulled her ponytail tighter. Her stupid heart jumped when she saw him. Even tired and haggard, he was the best-looking man she knew. "No, but I got a lecture on how fortunate I am to escape another surgery." She stared straight ahead at the large window that covered the wall. It was easier to pretend to focus on the view of the football field as she pumped along on the stationary bike than to look at Adrian. "Party too hard?" She was so lame.

"He was up all night with me. My leg was hurting really bad, and then he had a bunch of two-year-old horses with attitudes, and then he had to take me to the doctor, but not until he—"

"Mia, that's enough." He pulled his daughter close. "We're interrupting her workout."

"No. I'm fine." If she could, she would have hit

herself on the head. Adrian gave her an excuse to ignore them, but she had to be all agreeable.

Mia moved closer. "They say I might need another surgery." For a moment, concern flashed in the eyes of both father and daughter. "Hope I get to ride the bike today. It looks fun." And just like that, the sunshine smile was back on the adorable face.

The trainer walked in and saved Nikki from thinking of something appropriate to say. She watched in the mirrors that sat at an angle above the windows as Adrian shook hands with the petite brunette.

"Hi, Teresa."

"So, is Mia ready for the next step?" She gave the girl an encouraging look. "It won't be easy."

"I'm ready to do whatever it takes to get back on my horse. I want to ride in the July Jubilee."

Adrian's jaw muscles flexed and a glare sat hard in his eyes. "We've talked about this. You will not be riding in the rodeo. It doesn't matter what the doctor says. I'm your father, and I own that horse."

The sweet face of the ten-year-old suddenly held the same determined glare as her father's. Nikki couldn't help but smile. Adrian might not know it yet, but he was about to have his hands full with a preteen girl who wanted her horse back.

Nikki's father had been a roper, and she and her sisters grew up on the back of a horse. That was how he met Sheila, wife number two. Nikki's father had been blinded by the beautiful blonde and the idea of giving them a mother. He thought he was giving his daughters a mother and recapturing the family life they'd had with their mom. He'd learned the hard way that everything that glittered wasn't gold.

She had no right to judge. She'd made the same mistake.

Clearing her thoughts, she went back to watching Adrian as he hovered over Mia's physical therapist. It didn't seem as if he wanted to be married, not even to find a mother for his daughter and make his life easier. Any guy who gave up being a star in order to raise his daughter had to be a good man.

She'd dated some losers in the past. Maybe she could try a different kind of guy. A single-dad cowboy.

Ugh. What was she thinking? She leaned forward and closed her eyes, pretending she was outside, being challenged by a rocky terrain. Her knee protested, but she ignored it, pushing harder. She was tougher than the injury.

"Easy, Nikki." Teresa's lyrical voice pulled her from the trails on the north ridge. "We've talked about this. If you go too hard, you'll just set back your recovery. And according to your charts, you've been making striking progress. You need to give it some rest after the stress of the other day or all your hard work will be wasted and you'll have to start over. We don't want that, do we?"

Nikki grunted. She hated being talked to like she was a kid, especially from someone who was basically a kid herself. Leaning back on the seat, she slowed her pace and wiped her face with a towel.

Teresa was walking through the steps of how to use the bike with Mia when a teenage boy walked in. He had the look of an athlete and a shoulder brace. Teresa waved at him. "I'll be right there. Mia, I'm going to get Chris set up, so just take it slow." She glanced over at Nikki. "Would you mind keeping an eye on her?"

Great, the kid probably wanted to talk.

"I hate the way they keep saying to take it slow. I know it's my dad's fault."

She nailed that one. Nikki sighed. "So where did your father go?"

The thin shoulders lifted and then she faced Nikki, a small smirk forming on her lips. "Ms. Ortega had a talk with him. He was making us nervous. He'll be back to pick me up in about fifteen minutes. Then he can ask all the questions he wants. We will probably be here for another hour." She let out an exaggerated sigh.

"He loves you and is worried." Great, now she gave advice on dads. She was such a hypocrite.

"He says I'm never going to rodeo again." She frowned as she stared out the window. All the football players ran by on their way to the field.

"I doubt he really means it." Then again, what did she know?

"Will you help me? I think they're following my dad's orders to go easy on me, but at this rate, I'll never be ready for the July Jubilee rodeo." Her large eyes pleaded.

Nikki went back to watching the football players. They were running drills. The last thing she needed was to become the confidante to a ten-year-old against her dad. The silence must have clued Mia in on her doubts. The girl stopped spinning in place and turned to her. A full-on assault with the hurt puppy look.

"It's not fair. When he was my age, he rode bulls. I just want to run a horse around the barrels."

"At neck-breaking speeds." Nikki leaned her head back. This wasn't her problem. *Do not let it become your problem.*

The more she tried to ignore this little inner voice that told her she cared, the louder the sucking sound echoed in her head. Yep, the big brown eyes pulled her into a world she wanted no part of, ever.

"If I was a boy, he wouldn't do this to me."

And that was it. "If you're going to heal in record time, you can't stop moving." She gave a pointed glance to the feet not peddling. "Just keep working on getting better and show him how much you want to ride again. He'll come around."

The whirling sound of the stationary bike on the move picked up, and Mia pushed forward. "Do you think so? He can be stubborn. Even *Tío* thinks Daddy might not give on this one."

"I'm sure you can get your uncle George on your side."

The girl giggled. "I can threaten to use his whole name in public. It's Jorge Emilio Maria De La Cruz the fourth."

"Your uncle's middle name is Maria?"

A delightful giggle made Nikki smile.

"Great-grandpa came from Mexico. Maria is a common name for boys and girls. When Daddy is mad at my *tío*, he calls him Maria. Don't tell *Tío* I told you, or he will get upset with me. He claims there will not be a fifth."

"I won't say anything about the name. I can't make the same promise when it comes to your leg. What does your uncle think about you racing again?"

"He says he has to side with my dad, even if he disagrees." A sigh sounding too heavy for a ten-year-old escaped. "It was my first real rodeo, and now I'm afraid he won't let me go back. You'll help me work out and push me harder?"

Why wasn't she strong enough to look away from those big brown eyes? "Hey, we're workout buddies, right?"

Mia's face lit up, and just like that the joy was back. How did Adrian ever manage to tell her no? "Right." Leaning forward, her jaw went tight and determination flowed from every ounce of the small body and into the movements. "I wish I had a mom. She'd be able to handle my dad. That's what moms do, right?"

"You don't see your mom?" Her chest tightened. Why didn't she change the subject?

"Nope. Pretty much after giving birth to me, she took off. I know her name, but that's it. She gave up all her rights to me. I found a picture of her in an old yearbook. Daddy doesn't want to talk about her. He gets upset."

Now her stomach knotted. Memories, emotions and acid flooded her body. She gripped the handles and forced air in and out. Outside the window, clouds drifted by. She breathed in the soft white image and breathed out all the ugly of her life.

The panic attack would not win. The air pushed faster through the wheel turning in place. Faster and faster she pushed her legs. Sweat dripped from her body. Mia leaned forward as if they were in a race.

"Hey, easy!" Adrian's voice crashed into the wall she'd built and knocked a chunk out of the bricks.

"Daddy! You scared me. We're working to make our legs stronger." Mia looked at her dad then to Nikki. A silent begging filled the room.

"Your daughter is a hard worker. You should be proud of her, Adrian. At this rate, she should be more than ready to ride again by July. A concrete goal is a great motivator to work through the pain."

His lips tightened and he turned to Mia. "Go wash off and get yourself ready. We'll talk to Teresa before we leave."

Getting off the bike, Mia hugged her. "Thank you, Ms. Bergmann."

Her heart melted a bit and she sucked in a hard breath. She couldn't afford a soft heart. "Call me Nikki."

After Mia left, Adrian turned his full attention to her. He didn't look happy. "I'm not sure what you thought you were accomplishing by encouraging her to ride in the July rodeo, but it's not happening. I've been very clear, and she understands."

"I don't mean to step on any toes, but she's determined to ride in July. Your daughter doesn't understand why she can't ride if she's released by the doctor. Adrian, you were riding bulls at her age."

"It's different."

"Why? Because she's a girl?"

"She's my daughter. You're not a parent. You don't get how scary it is when you see your kid almost die in front of you."

You're not a parent. No, she had given up the right to be called by that name. The edges of her eyesight blurred as she tried to force the hot air out of her lungs. It didn't work. She sucked in through her nose. Grabbing the towel, she swung her leg over and got off the bike. "You're right. I overstepped. But your daughter asked for my help. So I don't think she's given up on the idea to ride again."

Jaw locked and spine straight, she turned away from him and lifted her bag onto her shoulder. She didn't dare pause to take a shower or wash off her face. Her hand was on the door when Mia caught up with her. *No, no, no.*

"What did my dad say?"

Without looking down, she stood on the threshold. "He says you're not riding. I've gotta go. See you later." A quick movement had the door closed to the little girl who was looking at her as if Nikki could give her something she wasn't capable of giving.

As fast as her limp would take her, she went to the edge of the sidewalk and looked for her father. Some of the students and teachers leaving campus waved at her. She didn't recognize most of them. Her father wasn't waiting for her. The breath froze in her lungs, and she focused on counting. He was never late. He had to be all right. She looked at her watch again. It was still early.

He was fine. A customer held him up. *Breathe.*

She cleared her mind of the terrible things that could happen to her father, and Mia took over. Those big eyes that went straight to her heart. She hoped she never saw Adrian's daughter again. It was too much to handle.

Everyone had a breaking point, and being in Clear Water might be hers. She needed a new plan that involved getting out of town as soon as possible.

It had been twelve years. Enough time for her to get over it. What was wrong with her? She hadn't had a panic attack in the last five or six years. Maybe longer. It was this town, and being around her family.

A horn beeped several times. Oh man, it was

Danica and the twins. They were all waving, too happy for a tragedy to have taken her dad.

Her breathing came in irregular patterns as Danica put her Accord in Park. Suzie rolled down the window, her twin pushing her way over her shoulder as Nikki got into the front passenger seat. Lizzy smiled so big and the sisters started talking at once, echoing each other just like Danica and Jackie did when they were growing up. Did they still finish each other's sentences?

"Hey, girls, slow down. We got some new baby bats at the sanctuary and they're excited." She turned to the girls. "You're freaking out your aunt." Danica smiled at Nikki, but there was concern in her eyes.

She tried to return the smile, but thinking about all she missed was overwhelming. Her nieces were six years old; her dad was getting older. Her son would be twelve soon.

Everything froze. Her lungs, her brain, the blood pumping to her heart. Adrian said she didn't understand being a parent. No, no, no. She couldn't go there. She couldn't.

A warm touch brought her attention back to the car as a large raindrop fell on her leg. No. Not a raindrop—a tear, her tear.

She buried her head in her hands. She couldn't lose it here, not in front of her young nieces.

"Nikki?" Her sister's voice shook. They had never seen her cry, even after their mother died. She made sure of it. She was the oldest. Her father and the twins needed her to be strong. Then Daddy married Sheila, making things worse.

She still needed to be strong.

"Girls, get your seat belts back on." Danica leaned over and hugged her. In a hushed voice, she spoke close to Nikki's ear. "I don't know what is going on, but you're going to let Jackie and me take care of you. I don't know why you've stayed away so long, but if it was something we did, you have to tell us so we can fix it. We love you."

Nikki nodded and glanced back at the identical girls in the back seat. Their dejected little faces looked so much like Dani's and Jackie's at that age. The image of them on the way to their mother's funeral.

They had been too little to really understand, but they knew life had forever been changed. Their father had gone numb, disappearing into himself. The woman that held his world together, the one he was going to grow old with, left them without warning. The dash of a panicked deer in front of her mom's car was all it took for her laughter and love to be gone forever. Leaving Nikki to take care of everyone. She wiped her face.

Then she'd messed up, believing a lie. She'd given all her love to the wrong boy. She couldn't keep it inside any longer. The time to tell her sisters the truth was close.

Adrian stared at the door Nikki disappeared through. He should apologize. When had he turned into one of those old grumpy cowboys?

The therapist, Teresa Ortega, took Mia to the table and wrapped ice on the hurt leg. She greeted him with a friendly expression.

"We were just talking about the timetable to get back on her horse. You have one determined young lady."

He needed to get the idea of barrel racing out of his daughter's head. Now he understood why his mother had refused to attend the shows after watching his first ride. She'd been at every one of them, but sat in the parking lot and waited for his ride to be over.

Maybe if he had been in the parking lot instead of watching from the railing, he could have had an easier time letting her back on her horse. The doctors said the deep sand of the arena saved her from a much worse injury, or even death. He couldn't get the image out of his head of that bright yellow ribbon flying as she pitched back and forth like a Ping-Pong ball.

"Daddy! Ms. Ortega says I'm impressive!"

He put his hand on the back of her neck, reassuring himself that she was fine and would heal. "You've always impressed me."

After several questions and instructions for the exercises Mia needed to complete at home, he got her secured in the truck. "Sorry about the church event, but you just got your cast off. I don't think you're ready for a rock-climbing trip."

Arms crossed, she leaned her forehead against the window and nodded. "I know." Defeat in her voice.

It was so much easier when she was younger. He dreaded her becoming a teenager. Glancing behind them, he checked for a clear path. Just like the side mirror, his gut told him they were much closer to the teen years than they appeared. He had to do something to make her feel better.

"Hey, bug, maybe we can have one of those tea parties when we get home?"

She rolled her eyes—not a good sign.

"Daddy, I'm too old for tea parties."

When had that happened? He tried to remember the last one. No one warned him time was up. He tried to remember the last time he carried her from the truck so she wouldn't wake up.

"Maybe your *tío* will let you paint his nails.

That's always fun. What about your new coloring books? I haven't colored in a while."

"Daddy, you're so silly. How about I color and you watch the game. The Spurs play tonight. We could invite some people over."

"Sure. You have some friends you want to call?" He turned the truck down the back road behind the school.

"Well, I was thinking more for you."

His head whipped in her direction. With her hands in her lap and looking straight ahead, she was trying too hard to look innocent.

"Me?"

"Daddy, why don't you ever date? *Tío* does. I know he hasn't found anyone that he likes for marrying, but at least he's trying. You don't go anywhere but work and my activities."

"What?" When did his daughter start taking note of his and George's social life? He was gonna have to talk to George about being more discreet. She was getting older and noticing things. Maybe if he just ignored it for right now, he would come up with a better answer later. How did a father talk to his daughter about dating? He had always told her she could ask him anything. He was rethinking that policy.

"Daddy, we could ask Nikki to come over. She's new in town, and she likes the Spurs. I know. I asked her, because I know how important that is to you."

His hand gripped the steering wheel as he turned down the caliche road to their house. "I think we should keep it to just us tonight. Why do you think I should be dating?"

She shrugged and pulled on invisible threads at the edge of her shirt. "It would be nice to have another girl around the house and to see you happy."

"I'm happy." He heard himself grumble. It had been them and George for her whole life. Parking in front of the barn, he watched as she climbed down from the side step of the truck and made her way to the house. She turned and looked at him, waiting for him to follow her. When had he become not good enough?

Chapter Five

The announcer called for the next event, pole bending. Mia sighed as if the world had ended. Now he wished he had found someone to cover the concession stand hours he signed up for at the beginning of the season. Being here seemed to torture her.

As a couple of boys ran off with giant pickles, she tightened the lid on the jar with another sigh. He poured heavy cheese sauce over corn chips and handed the four Frito pies to Katy Buchannan, making sure to smile. Hopefully it didn't look as fake as it felt.

She gave him that "oh, bless your heart" look he used to get all the time when he first became a single father. She leaned in and spoke low. "How's she doing? It must be so hard for her to be here."

Adrian took the money for the Frito pies and

Big Red sodas. "I think it might be harder for me than her, but we're good. They have her in physical therapy now. We're taking it slow, one day at a time."

"I hear you've been rescuing damsels in distress on Main Street. Maybe you'll finally have a date for the July Jubilee." The spark in her eyes and the girlish giggle warned him. That speculation of his love life gave her way too much enjoyment.

Oh man, the gossip mill is already grinding. He rubbed the back of his neck and glanced at his daughter to make sure she wasn't listening. "I think if Nikki heard you referring to her as a damsel in distress, you'd need to take cover. She's made it clear she doesn't need help, and I've never taken a date to the Jubilee. I don't need the complication. Nikki plans to be gone by then anyway." Which was a good thing for his peace of mind.

The young Bergmann twins Suzie and Lizzy skipped to the counter. Their mother came up behind them. Danica's red curls already ran loose from her braid. She smiled at Adrian. "We hoped you would help to convince my wayward sister to stay around. It's time for her to come home."

Katy laughed. "Did you hear he was spotted carrying her from my store?"

Danica winked at him. "I know. Isn't it adorable?"

The snack bar suddenly got warm, and Adrian pushed up his sleeves. He needed to find a way to stop this bull before it got out of the barn. The only problem was, as the women kept talking his mind stopped working.

"Mom! Can we get hamburgers?"

Now, there was a problem he could fix. "Sorry, girls. No burgers today, but I can make you Frito pies or nachos."

Danica looked past him. "Are you working by yourself?"

Katy leaned over the counter and scanned the area. "Oh, I'm sorry. I didn't even realize you were alone. Who signed up to work with you?"

"Vickie, but Ashley got sick. She came in and set everything up and then had to leave because Jake was going to work. I told her I could handle it as long as I didn't have to cook the hamburger patties too. Mia's not riding, so I'm fine."

"I'd help, but I have all four boys here. Speaking of which, I need to leave. See you later. We're praying for you, Mia."

Danica rested her elbows on the counter bar. The twinkle in her eye sent dread down his spine and into his gut. Her voice was low, so he had to lean in to hear her.

"Nikki's here. I'll put her in charge of the twins and come help you." She was digging money out of a huge leather bag. "Girls, you each get a dollar. Maybe you can come visit after your shift."

With the money in hand, they went to Mia to get a pickle.

"Really, you don't need to. It's not—"

"Stop right there. If you saw another parent working the shift alone, what would you do?"

That trap was set, and he knew there was no getting out of it. Without anything worth saying, he just looked at her, defeated. He had a feeling he would also be talking to Nikki before the day was over.

"Yeah, that's what I thought. Come on, girls." She looked at Adrian. "I'll be right back."

The girls stood on their toes to talk to Mia. "When do you get to ride again? Do you want to come see our new horse *Opa* bought us?" The Bergmann twins talked so fast it was hard to tell who said what.

"Daddy, can I just walk over with them? I won't get on a horse. I promise to just talk to my friends. I want to see their new horse and visit Rachel. Please, Daddy."

"You need to stay here."

"Adrian, she can come with me. I'll bring her back."

A group of teenage boys rushed the counter, wanting to buy drinks and candy. He nodded at Danica before giving his attention to the group of young ropers. He knew the burn in the pit of his stomach was based on unfounded fear. He closed his eyes for a second and took a deep breath. Mia would be walking across the rodeo grounds with Danica. Nothing was going to happen.

As he pulled four bottles out of the cooler, his daughter wrapped her small arms around him and pressed her cheek against his back. "Thank you, Daddy. I'll be careful." And with that, she was out of the concession stand, waving to the boys as she walked past them on her crutches.

The boys all smiled as she giggled. Adrian narrowed his eyes. The day he had to worry about boys was approaching too fast. He was starting to miss his little girl already.

He wasn't ready for this new phase of life. He glanced over the boys' shoulders as he took their money. Mia was laughing as she followed Danica through the small crowd. Nope, his little girl was getting older and more than her broken leg was the problem. If he couldn't keep her from breaking bones, how could he even begin to know how to protect her heart? He gave each boy a hard glare. Not sure why, but it made him feel better.

"Did you ride when you were young?" Mia leaned in closer to Nikki as they sat on the lowest bleacher. They chatted about horses as they waited for the twins to take their new horse through the poles. A girl Nikki didn't know ran first. The flying lead changes were beautiful to watch. She couldn't imagine the girls riding that fast.

"I was four the first time I was out on a horse by myself." Now that seemed impossibly young. She tried to remember when she started craving the speed. Maybe around nine or ten, but it all blurred together.

She did remember when jumping from cliff tops and taking on white-water rapids replaced horses. Maybe her ex was right and she was trying to find her breaking point.

She smiled down at her unexpected physical-therapy partner. "I was on the back of a horse every day until I started playing sports in middle school. I started splitting time, but rode whenever I could. We would hit as many rodeos as we could get to on the weekend. My dad used to rope, so it was a family event." Until her dad married Sheila and messed everything up, but a ten-year-old didn't need to hear those stories. Other than the girl might need to know that she was better off without a mother than being stuck with a bad mother. Not every woman was designed to care for children.

"There you are. It's time to go home." From behind her, the deep calm voice she tried to forget penetrated her consciousness, derailing all her other thoughts.

Why did Adrian De La Cruz get under her skin more so than any man in her past? If she didn't turn around maybe he would walk right past her and focus on his daughter. He had said it was time to leave.

"Daddy, Rachel's next and then Lizzy and Susan will be coming up. Please can we watch?"

Nikki's dad sat on the other side of Mia, taking pictures with a crazy long lens. The only empty spot was the one right next to Nikki. Adrian slid onto the edge of the metal bench. She scooted closer to Mia. A rumbling sound came from his throat. Did he just growl?

She kept her focus straight ahead and tried to ignore the way the rough sound tickled the nerves along her spine. It wasn't meant to be a good sound. He was probably thinking of the last time they had talked. It had ended with him being mad at her. It wasn't her fault if he was uptight and sexist when it came to his daughter. She straightened her spine.

Adrian shook his head in what looked like disgust. "I can't believe they have Cooper on that horse. That mare is crazy. She's too hot for a six-year-old."

Nikki's father agreed with a nod. "I told Peterson that horse was too much for his grandson. The kid's only six, but the idiot has to prove everyone wrong."

Relief that it wasn't her he growled at softened her back. Then she saw what upset Adrian and her father.

The powerful buckskin made the redheaded boy look small, too small to handle the horsepower under the miniature saddle. The boy pulled hard on the reins and the big mare tossed her head. The muscles in her massive neck and chest bunched as she pawed the ground. The kid looked scared with a death grip on the saddle horn. His grandfather Jim Peterson walked out. Maybe he was going to lead them out of the arena. Instead he popped the horse on the rear and yelled at the boy. "Show her who's boss, Cooper."

The horse lunged, and the six-year-old leaned over the saddle horn, now both hands hanging on as if he was going to fall. Adrian muttered something under his breath and stood. Nikki looked back at the boy. His eyes shut tight, he wasn't even looking as the horse took the first pole and started weaving through them on autopilot.

At the last pole the mare turned right instead of left. The boy's eyes opened, and he pulled hard on the reins as he tried to turn the horse back on the correct pattern. The big buckskin threw her head and twisted the opposite direction.

Nikki stood with everyone else in the stands as the horse lost balance and went down. With both hands on the saddle horn, Cooper stayed in the saddle even as the horse popped back up, but the boy lost the reins.

With no way to control the animal, he clung to the saddle horn as the leather reins flew, out of reach. With one hand reaching out, Cooper grabbed for the lost strap. The horse came to a quick stop and reared. He lost his balance and landed on the sandy area floor. The horse looked even bigger as it came down and went back up, front hooves striking out.

Adrian was over the panel and running to the boy. Nikki grabbed the top railing to follow but her father put his hand on her shoulder. "With your leg, you'll just be in the way."

She gritted her teeth. He was right. So she watched, helpless, from the sidelines as Adrian scooped the small body into his arms and shielded the boy from danger with his back to the horse. A few other cowboys joined him, herding the now-crazed horse away from the boy. Gwyn, Cooper's mother, came running.

"Cooper! Oh, baby! Cooper?" The petite blonde struggled through the deep sand.

Adrian had got to the side of the arena near Nikki. A couple of the other guys corralled the white-eyed mare on the opposite side.

Yelling and sobbing, Gwyn reached for her son, who was now clinching Adrian's neck and crying. Mia moved past Nikki and down the steps to the small gate by the bleachers.

Nikki noticed the tear in Adrian's shirt. The horse's front hooves must have caught his shoulder. She reached for her medical bag then gritted her teeth in realization. All she had was a useless purse. Not even a basic first-aid kit.

She and her father followed Mia. "Fool man. Peterson could've gotten his grandson killed. Good thing Adrian's so fast." Her father grumbled on, but she was focused on Gwyn and Adrian.

Adrian's mouth was moving, but he was speaking so low she couldn't hear him.

The whole county could hear Gwyn. "Thank you. Thank you, Adrian. You saved his life," she managed between sobs as she hugged Adrian and Cooper.

Mr. Peterson joined them, leading the hard-breathing horse. "Boy, you need to get back on this horse. Not good for a horse to think this is the way it goes. It's a bad lesson."

"No, Daddy. Cooper should've never been on her to begin with." She took her son from Adrian. "She's your horse. You ride her."

Cooper's grandfather looked as if he was about to argue.

Going through the gate, Nikki noticed Adrian square up to Gwyn's father. Glancing around the arena, it didn't look as if many of the other cowboys were happy about the boy being put back on the horse.

With a grunt, he mounted the horse and turned her to the gate. Gwyn stayed focused on her son. The crying had stopped. Nikki was relieved to see they had gained some control. Other than some sand in his hair, the boy was untouched.

Adrian, on the other hand, was not. "Let me treat the wound," she said.

He scowled at her as if he had no clue what she was talking about. "I'm fine."

"Your back is bleeding. The hoof must have sliced through your shirt." She moved to get a closer look.

Gwyn gasped. "Oh no. You're hurt." She started crying again. "That could have been Cooper's little head!"

He glared at Nikki as if the woman's emotional outbreak was her fault. "I'm fine, and more importantly Cooper is good. Mia, why don't you take them over to the back of the concession stand and help them get the sand out of Cooper's hair, and something to eat and drink? My treat. Gwyn, it's all good." Mia nodded and opened the small gate, waiting for them to join her. Gwyn gave him another hug before following Mia.

"Now that they're getting taken care of, I need to assess your injury." Nikki stepped closer to him. "At the very least, it needs to be cleaned and covered. It might even need stitches. Do they have a first-aid kit here?"

He twisted his neck trying to see, his right hand pulling his shoulder forward. Jake Torres, the new sheriff, walked across the arena as if he owned it. She shook her head. He was the sheriff now and married to Vickie. Leave for a few years and the world turned upside down.

"I wish I could arrest people for stupidity. How bad is it? Do I need to call the ambulance?" Jake asked.

Adrian glared at him. "You do that, and you'll need it more than I do."

Men, they were the biggest babies. "It needs a cleaning. Without a good look, I don't know how deep it is. Do you have a first-aid kit?"

"Yep. In my truck. Come on, and we'll get this done." Jake turned and walked through the small gate. Danica was there.

"I was with the girls and heard Adrian saved Cooper. Is everyone all right?"

Adrian sighed. "Cooper is good. Mia took them to the concession stand to clean him up. I'm going over there to help. Then I'm going home." He looked at Nikki. "I'll make sure to wash as soon as I get home." He glanced at her knee. "You shouldn't be on your feet without your crutches."

"Thanks, Dad." She took a deep breath and smiled. Sarcasm was not needed right now. "A horse's shoe cut through your shirt and skin. Take a minute to imagine all the stuff that could be wedged between the metal and hoof." With hands on her hips, she gave him a minute to process that information. "It needs to be cleaned. If it was your daughter, would you wait until you got home to clean it? I was a medic with the navy. Let me clean it and see if you need more."

He crossed his arms but dropped them quickly. His jaw tightened. "You want me to take my shirt off right here?"

She tried to stop her eyes from rolling. "No.

I want you to go to Jake's horse trailer with me. You don't even have to take off your shirt. I just need to see the back of that left shoulder, unless you have other injuries you haven't told us about."

Jake shook his head and started walking to the trailers. "Stop whining and come on."

Sammi came up on the other side of Adrian. "Dad has a couple of shirts in the trailer. Want me to get one?"

"I'm fin—"

"That's a good idea." Her little sister took off to retrieve a clean shirt.

"It's better than the boy having blood on him." Adrian grumbled a few other words.

She touched his arm and he jerked away. "Hey, I know it's hard to be the one who needs help. I'm the queen of refusing it, but just recently someone came to my aid and I would like to return the favor."

"Let the lady take care of you, Adrian. Not sure why you're being so stubborn about her looking at your injury." Jake looked at Adrian's closed face then back at her and shrugged.

When they arrived at the large silver gooseneck trailer, Jake pulled a five-gallon bucket from the living quarters in the front of it. A small group of people had gathered around them. Nikki's skin tightened as the crowd started asking questions and getting closer. Maybe this was why Adrian just wanted to leave.

Jake chased everyone off and pulled out a red box from his truck. "This should have everything you need."

Vickie came rushing over. "Oh, my! I saw the whole thing. I was with Ashley, who is feeling better, getting her ready to run. That was amazing, Adrian. When Cooper fell under that horse, I just—"

"Where is Ashley now?" Jake stopped her from talking and nodded at Nikki over Adrian's shoulder. "I think Nikki has this covered. Let's go make sure everything is running smooth again."

Nikki's gut tightened as she watched Jake take Vickie's hand. Being around Vickie was too difficult. How did you tell someone their children had a half brother?

She thought she heard them say goodbye, but she needed to focus on Adrian. Putting on gloves, she got the scissors out and removed enough of the shirt to see the cut. "Sorry about the shirt." There was so much uncertainty, her head hurt. She kept doing what she knew how to do, clean and dress a wound.

Adrian's jaw tightened as his breathing came faster. He leaned to the side and tried to look around the trailer. "Can you see Mia? She's not around the horses, is she?" He went to stand, but she put pressure on the top of his good shoulder. He gave a low growl. "I shouldn't have sent her off alone."

"She's fine, and she's not alone. You have a great daughter. She wanted to help, just like her father, and you gave her something productive to do." Nikki bit down on her lip.

He gave another glance over his shoulder. His skin was clammy and a bit pale. Oh man, he'd seen his daughter being dragged by a horse not that long ago.

This must have brought him back to that horrific moment. "Adrian, she's okay. Today you relived a traumatic event, and I've seen that sorta thing break down the toughest guys. It had to be hard for you. So do whatever you need to do to get it out of your system. It's just you and me."

His jaw flexed and his eyes narrowed as he stared off beyond the trailer. No words.

"You responded so fast, that little boy doesn't have a scratch because of you." That was why Jake had cut Vickie off and got her out of there. She had been so caught in her own personal drama she'd been clueless to his state of mind. She took a deep breath. "Do you need to talk about it?" She didn't know what else to say. She'd never been good at emotional stuff, but she knew it had helped some of the guys to talk to someone who was safe.

He grunted. "I'm fine." His jaw did double time and he closed his eyes. "Cooper should have never been on that horse."

Using the antibacterial wipes, she cleaned the angry cut that ran across the top of his shoulder blade. Giving him the silence he needed if he wanted to say something.

"Mia is not getting back on a horse," he managed through gritted teeth.

Not what she was hoping to hear. "It must have been horrible to watch and not get to her fast enough."

"Everyone thinks I'm overreacting. The other day you pretty much said the same thing." He sucked in a quick breath as she hit a sensitive spot.

"Sorry. The good news is we can patch you up with some butterfly bandages. No stitches needed. Infection is your strongest threat. It's bruised pretty badly, so it's going to be sore, but the bone feels fine."

"You didn't answer my question. Do you think I'm overreacting when it comes to Mia?"

This was the problem with encouraging people to talk. They did, and then they wanted you to talk. The sincerity she saw in the leather-brown eyes turned her insides to liquid. She leaned closer.

A light knock on the end of the trailer saved her from saying anything. She had never been so happy to see her sister. Sammi poked her head around the trailer. "Is it safe?"

Normally friendly Adrian glared at her sister. "Why wouldn't it be?"

"Oh, I don't know." Sam had a blue-collared shirt draped over her arm, and Danica was behind her. "You saved her the other day, and now she got to save you."

"You're a perfect match." Danica grinned and wiggled her eyebrows.

From the other side of the trailer, George joined them. "So this is where you're hiding? Y'all are taking turns playing damsel in distress? Sounds like a fun game."

"No." Nikki's voice squeaked.

"I'm not a damsel." Adrian's deep low voice matched her higher one. She hated it when her voice did that. George, Sammi and Danica laughed at them. She loathed being laughed at.

Apparently so did Adrian. The glare he shot his brother was lethal. "You need to stop right now. I'm not hurt enough that I can't shut you up, Maria."

His twin didn't seem bothered by the threat. "Oh, this is bad if you're pulling out my middle name. So you were playing the hero again? There's already talk of banning Gwyn's father for the play day. People are saying you jumped in front of the horse and saved Cooper's life." George shook his head. "Always got to be the hero. Thanks, Nikki, for being there to carry him off if needed." He grinned at her. She knew physically it was the exact same grin as Adrian's, but it didn't do the trick to her heartbeat that his twin's did.

"George, leave her alone. She was a medic in the navy, so she's doing what she does." Adrian's jaw had gone all hard again.

This was one of the reasons she hated small towns. Everyone thought they had the right to talk about you.

George moved so he could see Adrian's back. "Not bad. He's had worse." He turned to Nikki. "Thanks for making him sit and take his medicine. I know it wasn't easy."

Adrian rolled his shoulder and groaned. It was low but she heard it. She went into the bag for painkillers. He was always forcing them on her. Now it was her turn.

With a hand on her shoulder, George got her attention. She had tuned out the conversation and didn't know what he was talking about.

"—you should come."

Danica actually clapped. "What a great idea.

It's tomorrow night and you can go with me and Jackie."

She looked at Adrian for help.

"You should come. Tomorrow George and I are hosting the monthly single parents' social."

Okay, so she would go for the obvious. "I'm not a single parent."

George winked. "I'm not either, but when you're a single twin of a single parent, you're in by default. Since you're the single sister of twins, I say you are welcomed. It's what happens when you live in a small town." He patted Adrian on his good shoulder. "So, we'll see you there. You deserve a juicy well-cooked steak for putting up with his sorry attitude."

Adrian crossed his arms, but grimaced and immediately dropped them again. "You weren't here and have no idea what kind of attitude I had."

George slid his hands into his front pockets and leaned against the trailer. "Oh, I can only imagine, and it wasn't anywhere near gracious and kind."

Why was he giving Adrian such a hard time? "He was fine. Other than being worried about Cooper and Mia, Adrian was a model patient."

Danica laughed and George raised an eyebrow. "Your time with the navy must have given you a different idea of a model patient." George straightened and dusted something off his pants she couldn't see. "We'll see you tomorrow." He gave Danica a quick hug before looking back at Adrian. "I'll grab our rug rat and head home. Take as much time as you need to finish up here."

Sammi stepped forward and hung the shirt on the edge of the canopy. "I'll leave the shirt here."

Danica wrapped her arms around their little sister. "The girls have one more run, then we'll load up the horses. Adrian, do you mind taking Nikki home? I'm sure this has been too much for her. She's standing all stiff like she's in pain." Without waiting for a response from either of them, she turned and disappeared around the trailer with Sammi.

"Sorry about that." Nikki forgot how annoying it was to be around people who thought they knew you better than you knew yourself.

"She's right. You need to get home and get off your feet." He stood and took the borrowed shirt off the coat hanger. "I'll slip inside and change shirts. Then we can go home. Do you need any painkillers?"

Now that everyone brought it to her attention, she could feel the throbbing of her knee. "No, I'm fine, but what about you? Should you be driving?"

He snorted. "I've driven with cracked ribs

and fractured bones. I don't think a cut is going to slow me down." He stepped into the living quarters of the large horse trailer, but stopped and turned back to her. His arm braced on the door frame. "Nikki, thank you."

For a quick second, his lips tightened. "For everything. And the other day I said some things I wanted to apologize for. When I first became a dad, people were telling me how I didn't know this or that. They treated me like an idiot because I was such a young father. I'd get mad."

His boots now had his full attention. "Then I heard myself telling you the same thing." Looking up, he gave her that lopsided grin that melted her stupid heart. "I was wrong. You were right about something. I do have a great daughter, but I don't know how to let her be independent and keep her protected at the same time. And today…well, today didn't help my state of mind."

Throwing the shirt over his good shoulder, he straightened. "Anyway, thanks." He closed the door.

She was in so much trouble. How had Adrian stayed single for so long? How had Mia's mother walked out on him and not looked back?

Focus, Nikki. Stay focused. Would he understand if she told him about the decision she made as a seventeen-year-old? She let herself imagine how things would be different if he had been the father of her son instead of Tommy. Would they have told her family together? Would she have kept her son? She shook her head, resisting the urge to hit it against the metal trailer. The past was the past and it couldn't be changed.

It was time to tell her family. She wasn't a scared teenager who feared hurting the ones she loved. If she was really honest, rejection made her want to hide.

Maybe it was a bit of pride too. She had been the big sister who kept everything together. How would they treat her if she confessed to falling down?

All she knew was that the secret created a hole in her gut. Maybe this was the real reason she came home.

Her sisters said God brought her home for something special. She had a hard time thinking God cared enough about her small life to arrange this homecoming. But did He? What she did know was it was time to bring the truth out into the light of day. Maybe it would help her finally be free of the past.

With his palms flat against the wall of the small sleeping quarters, Adrian pushed his weight into his arms. He dropped his head.

His eyes shut tight. He took deep breaths. He couldn't fall apart every time he saw a kid in danger of being hurt. Nikki had seen through him, but he didn't think anyone else saw the extent of his trauma. Jake might have seen it. He ushered Vickie out and left him alone with Nikki.

He arched his back before starting to unbutton his ruined shirt. Nikki understood. She hadn't poked or pushed. She just gave him the space and time he needed. He flinched as he pulled the clean shirt over his head.

Mia was going to go crazy if he kept this up. He knew he had to give her some freedom or he would lose her, but she was only ten. Maybe he should talk to Pastor John. He had a teen daughter and faced problems that overwhelmed a single dad.

He stepped out and paused. Nikki packed the first-aid kit, her movements efficient and graceful. It would be so much easier if he had a partner, a woman's perspective, as he entered this new territory with his daughter.

Everyone seemed to have a not-so-subtle plan to match them up. If Nikki planned to stay, she would be the kind of woman he would want around his daughter, strong and independent.

He must have made some noise because she looked up and smiled. "That color looks good on you. You should wear that shade of blue more often." She stood and wiped her hands. "You don't have to give me a ride home. I can wait for the family."

As she put the box back in the lower compartment, he noticed she favored her injured leg. "You need to elevate and ice your knee. Did you take any of those painkillers you were peddling to me?" He moved to the small door and closed it, looking her in the eye as he waited for the answer.

She turned away from him and shrugged. "As I've been told several times today—" after a few steps away from him, she turned back and made eye contact "—I'm fine." Her eyes looked a darker blue today, reminding him of a storm rolling over the hills. "You know they're trying to set us up. I think your daughter's even in on it. Do you get this a lot?"

He settled his hat back on his head. "Nope. Not lately, anyway. They gave up a few years ago. Writing me off as a lost cause. I guess they see us as the perfect lost-cause couple." He grinned.

Nikki crossed her arms. "It's not funny. I think they're offering you up as bait to get me to stay here."

A chuckle rattled around his chest, but the pain cut it short. He did love her humor. "If I was you, I'd be insulted if I'm all they have to offer you with. A single dad, washed-up bull rider that has commitment issues. They set the bar low." He studied the emotions she tried to hide as she avoided his gaze. She was a puzzle, confident but vulnerable at the same time.

She rubbed her leg then stood. "You're cute in that washed-up-bull-rider way. Okay, I'll take that offer of a ride home as long as we're clear that I'm leaving as soon as my leg is better."

"I'm cute?" He rubbed his jaw and the stubble felt like low-grade sandpaper.

"Oh, give me a break." With her hands on her hips, she rolled her eyes. "Like you haven't been told that a million times."

He liked the way she handled everything so straightforwardly. He nodded and offered his arm. "Your carriage awaits."

With a shake of her head, her few loose curls danced around her face. "Oh no. You've already been spotted carrying me. I can walk on my own free will with a good four feet between us. No more of this damsel-in-distress talk."

"Yes, ma'am." He hadn't had this much fun with a woman in a long time. Maybe there was a way to keep her in town. Dating took too much energy and time away from Mia, the horses and the old houses he restored. Now there was a woman who piqued his interest, and she made it clear he needed to keep his distance. *God, You have a twisted sense of humor.*

Once they got past the trailers, she started limping again. Why did she refuse the crutches? He carefully slipped an arm around her as she stiffly moved to his truck. She gave a slight grunt, but she didn't say anything about the four-foot rule.

He grinned. She was his kind of stubborn.

Chapter Six

Nikki tossed the end of the soft pink scarf over her shoulder. "I don't know why you think I need to wear more color. I like my gray T-shirt."

Danica handed her a tube of matching lipstick. "Here. You have beautiful lips, but they're fading into the rest of your skin."

The other twin nodded. "You're gorgeous. I don't understand why you don't want to look your best. It's not like we're making you fix your hair and change all of your clothes. It's a scarf and lipstick. Well, maybe a bit of mascara. It'll make your eyes stand out. I always wished we had your eye color." Jackie pulled out a green tube of what Nikki assumed was the marvelous thicker-lashes-in-one-swipe goop.

"My hair? What's wrong with my hair?" She didn't remember the twins being this bossy. "I thought this was a simple church social for single parents. Which I would like to point out, again, I'm not." Giving birth didn't count.

"Single parents. Like Adrian." Her sisters giggled like middle schoolers.

Sammi, their youngest sister, sat on the edge of the bed with her arms crossed. "I don't know why you're trying to set her up with Adrian. She's told us she's leaving. And I don't understand why I can't go. Just like Nikki said, she and Jackie aren't single parents. You're just single like me."

Danica sat next to her and put an arm around the stiff shoulders. "We aren't trying to set her up with anyone. We're just having fun. It's been so long since we got to do sister things with her. You're too young. You'd be bored with all us old folks."

"I'm twenty-one." She scowled as the three older sisters laughed.

"Oh, sweetheart. Someone needs to stay here with Daddy and the girls anyway. He's been acting weird lately." Jackie hugged her and kissed Sammi's forehead.

"Come on—let's go." Danica headed out the door without looking back.

Nikki offered a hand out to Sammi and pulled her up into her arms. The last time she'd hugged her little sister, she had only been nine years old. Now she was a grown woman. "Sorry they're being so obnoxious. Tomorrow just you and I will do something. We have a lot of catching up to do."

"So when you leave this time, do you promise to come back?"

The weight of regret made her shoulders heavy. She tucked a strand of loose hair behind Sammi's ear. "I promise, kiddo." She bumped her forehead like they did when she was little. "I'll be back." The silly voice she used made Sam laugh. "At least once a year, I promise. And you can come see me. Have you rappelled down cliffs or hit white rapids?"

With a shake of her head, Sam smiled. "Sounds fun. Maybe we can go kayaking. Nothing so exciting around here. I would love to visit you."

"Nikki! We're gonna be late!" Danica yelled from downstairs.

One more hug, and Nikki went down to get in the old family Suburban. "I can't believe Dad still has the green beast." She got in the middle bench.

"Hey, it hit 400,000 miles. It just got broken in. Plus, it has a new transmission. He's not getting rid of it now." The girls chatted all the way out to Adrian's place. It was down Childress Ranch Road next to his parents' property. It wasn't far from her mother's family ranch.

She took a deep breath, not sure why she was so nervous. This was not a date. It was a church social.

There were all sorts of cars and trucks parked along the caliche drive. She hadn't expected this many people.

"Wow, this is a big turnout. And it looks as if we're late." Danica cut a glare to Nikki in the rearview mirror.

"What? Y'all are the ones who wanted to add color to me." She refused to feel guilty for spending a few extra moments with Sammi.

Danica moved to the back of the Suburban. "I'll get the brownies if one of you will grab the potato salad."

Nikki rushed to get the side dish. It would give her something to focus on other than the fear of whom she would see and what questions they'd ask her. She should have stood her ground and stayed home. The last thing she needed was to be around Adrian or anyone from Clear Water, but at least it was just the single parents. She didn't have to worry about seeing Vickie.

She followed her sisters then stopped to take in the building at the end of the long gravel drive. "That's a barn. Adrian lives in a barn?"

In unison the twins turned back and looked at her. "Not just a barn." They replied in stereo.

Danica sighed. "It was one of the Childress's old barns. Some great-great-grandparent built it. It wasn't used anymore and Dub was tired of the upkeep. Everyone thought Adrian was crazy for moving it here. Story is Dub sold it to him for a hundred bucks. And Adrian had to pay to move it. That was fun. The whole county came out to watch."

They turned their backs to her and started walking to the giant three-story barn that was lit up like an airstrip. Jackie continued the tale. "Everyone thought Adrian was crazy, including George. That was eight years ago. Now they all want to find a barn to convert. People are always asking to have weddings and parties here."

They approached the huge open sliding barn doors. The space inside was wide-open with over thirty people grouped in different areas. A pool table and several mix-matched farm tables were scattered around the room. At one end, a large river rock fireplace dominated the wall. The design flowing up like the Frio River itself. Instead of a fire, some kind of lamp lit the area.

Several people greeted them. Nikki didn't know there were this many unattached adults in Clear Water, let alone single parents.

"Hey, ladies!" George greeted them. "Yay! The Bergmann Brownies and potato salad.

They can go over to the side table." He winked at Nikki. "Adrian's out by the grill."

A group around one table started yelling and laughing. She raised an eyebrow to George. He laughed. "A game of spoons can get very competitive. They've been known to draw blood, so you've been warned if you join them."

Danica leaned into George. "Why are there people from the young-couples group?"

Nikki had to bite back a laugh. The definition of *young couple* was a bit liberal in Clear Water. A few of the couples were older than her and the rest were her age. The pastor was there. She had a hard time imagining Lorrie Ann Ortega as a pastor's wife, but she guessed that proved anything was possible. He certainly looked at her as if she was the only one in the room.

Nikki turned away from them before she got nauseous, only to find Vickie with Jake's arm draped over her shoulder.

A fine layer of sweat coated her skin. She had thought she'd be safe at a single parents' gathering. It seemed their use of the word *single* was a bit liberal also.

"Oh, you noticed our population explosion." He nodded and pointed to a pretty brunette by the fireplace. "Anjelica and Garrett were hosting the couples' social at their house tonight, but the old house had an electrical issue. So while her father and brothers are fixing it, Pastor John thought it would be fun for all of us to get together." He turned to Nikki. "Some of the married couples used to be part of our group, so now it's a twentysomething, thirtyish or forty-ish get-together."

Lorrie Ann's cousin, Anjelica, sat on a winged-back chair, talking with a woman Nikki didn't recognize. A tall, brooding man leaned across the back of her chair and kept looking at his watch. He seemed as uncomfortable as Nikki felt.

George moved in close and whispered in her ear. "It's their first date night without the kids. He's worried, and I don't think they're gonna last long." Well, she'd keep an eye on them—that way she wouldn't be the first to leave.

She had to get away from all these couples. Jackie took the dish from her and left her standing alone with George. The table erupted again in shouts and laughter.

They were having too much fun for her. She looked out the back door. That was one of the things she loved about the Grand Canyon. A person could go miles without seeing another body if they planned it right.

"Hey, come with me." Adrian's twin tilted his head to the escape she had already been eyeing. "I need to check the steak and chicken. I can't leave my little brother alone with them too long, or he'll dry them out." He shuddered.

Following him through the wide barn doors at the back, she found a rock patio that extended out a good ten feet with a short wall surrounding it. Several chairs and a couple of rocking chairs invited her to sit and stare at the night sky. This was a place straight out of her dreams she had for a home one day that she would build...in Arizona.

Laughter drifted from the darkness, drawing her attention away from the stars. Down the path, under a giant oak tree strung with hundreds of white lights, Adrian stood at a metal grill. Gwyn stood with him. Nikki looked back to the open doors of the barn turned house and tried to figure out which place would be the less excruciating. She could go sit in the Suburban and wait for her sisters.

"Nikki?" Adrian's voice called out to her. "Glad you decided to join us. I got the impression you weren't coming."

Gwyn stepped a little closer to Adrian. "It's been so long since you've visited, we thought you were never coming back. I'm sure your sisters are happy to see you."

She closed her eyes and tilted her head back. *Really, God.* She didn't want to talk to Adrian, especially with Gwyn.

"They aren't the only ones." George walked past her and stood next to his twin. With an elbow, he hit his brother. "Right?"

Adrian frowned at him and poked him back. "Lots of people are happy to see her."

"So how's Cooper doing?" Nikki needed to change the subject. "Has he recovered from his ordeal?"

Gwyn took the opportunity to touch Adrian on his arm. "Yes, and it's all due to Adrian's fast action. When I saw that horse fall. Then Coop dropped the..." Tears started welling up in her eyes. Adrian put his arm around her.

Nikki knew she had a strong skeptic streak, but she fought back the face she wanted to make. That would just make her look a bit on the rude side. George didn't seem to have the same concern. With a tilt of his head, he gave her an exaggerated eye roll.

Of course, he was standing over the grill. Behind his brother's shoulder where Nikki was the only one who could see him. He was going to get her in trouble. If she started laughing, Adrian and Gwyn might take offense.

Gwyn wrapped one arm around Adrian's shoulder. He stiffened.

Nikki stopped herself from stepping forward and checking his wound. "How's the cut? Do you need it rebandaged?" Why did she even offer? The last thing he needed was two women hovering over him.

Gwyn moved back. "Oh, I'm so sorry. I forgot you were injured. Did I hurt you?"

"I'm fine." He gave Nikki a sheepish look.

"Oh, buddy, I've heard that before. Let me see if you've reopened my handiwork." She moved to stand behind him and he blocked her by turning.

A long metal spatula in hand, George pointed it at his brother. "There is blood on your shirt."

A growl rumbled from Adrian's throat as he glared at his brother. "You stay out of this."

"Oh, Adrian, I'm so sorry! I didn't mean to hurt you all over again." Gwyn put her hand on his good shoulder and turned him and looked at the damage. "Your brother's right. There's blood on the shirt."

"There's a first-aid kit upstairs in the kitchen," George told them. "Y'all get him fixed. On your way in, could you send Jake out here to help me get the steaks and chicken in to everyone?"

Adrian moved closer to the grill, slipping out of Gwyn's reach. "I can help with the steaks."

"No offense, baby brother, but no one wants to be served by a bleeding hero." He waved them on. "Thanks, Nikki, for patching up my brother again."

"I want to help." Gwyn grabbed Adrian's arm

again and pulled him toward the house. "I might not be a nurse, but I've had experience putting boys back together. You saved my Cooper. Let me help you." Did she actually bat her eyes at him? Nikki didn't know women did that in real life. It made her stomach a little sour. It was really none of her business if Adrian liked the helpless-girl act.

Hanging back with George, she thought of all the ways she could leave. They didn't need a third wheel. She'd played that game before and she wasn't going there again. "I'll help George. Gwyn has it under control. Adrian doesn't need me."

"Hey, Gwyn! What do you know about stitches?" George called out.

Gwyn stopped and looked back at Adrian. "You have stitches? Oh no, was it that bad?"

Adrian's growl could be heard through the darkness that separated them. "I'm fine. I don't have stitches." Each word slipped through gritted teeth.

"Yeah, because Nikki knows how to do a killer butterfly bandage!" George yelled across the lawn. He flipped the steaks. "He would have been worse if she hadn't taken care of him." He turned to her. "Do you want your work to be undone?"

She sighed. If Adrian didn't want her help,

she wasn't going to force herself on him. She thought of him carrying her in the rain at the ranch and later on Main Street in front of the store. He was the one who did the forcing and she wasn't going to stoop to his level, even if he was too dense to know he needed her help. He wanted Gwyn to fix him up, that was fine with her.

"He's a grown man. He doesn't want my help."

"Nikki!" Adrian called her. "It feels like they've come undone. Would you mind replacing them?"

She put a smile on her face and joined them. The three of them walked through the large social area and up the stairs to the living quarters. Adrian must like open space, because the kitchen was only separated from the living area with an island made of stained concrete. It served as an eating counter on one side with four tall stools. The largest leather sectional she'd ever seen took up most of the space, anchored by an area rug of neutral colors. The wood floors shone. It was very masculine and comfortable.

She instantly wanted to curl up and stay. The woodwork, from huge beams above their heads to the details on the railing and walls, was amazing. Old pulleys and doors were used in creative ways. The coffee table was an old barn door. Pictures of Mia growing up showed through a pane of glass placed on top of the wooden squares.

The love of old buildings and wood was showcased in this remodeled barn. To the right was a spiral staircase leading to a loft. Colorful streamers of pink, purple and bright greens looked out of place. They created a wall for the upstairs room.

Nikki smiled. That had to be Mia's room.

Adrian sat on one of the bar stools. Gwyn hovered close by. "I hope I'm not the reason it started bleeding again."

Adrian sighed. "I'm sure it was something I did. Nikki, the first-aid kit is above the refrigerator."

"What do you need me to do?" Gwyn was now holding Adrian's hand as if he was a six-year-old. "I'm so sorry you got hurt. Watching Coop go down, then you blocked that horse from thrashing him. It was amazing. You were so brave and fast. Have you seen anything like it before, Nikki?"

Did the woman really expect her to reply? Sitting behind him, she pulled the collar of his button-up shirt below the shoulder and stayed focused on the wound. Gently pulling the old crisscross bandages off so she wouldn't cause more damage.

She hit the tender spot and Adrian flinched. He didn't move again, but he started talking. "Nikki was a medic in the navy and then worked with extreme adventures at the Grand Canyon. I'm sure for her this was no big deal."

"Are you sure you don't need me to get anything?" The woman's voice was like a fly that wouldn't go away. "Let me at least get you some water."

With everything finally back in place, Nikki stood. "That should hold it together for now. With you being so active, you might want to get stitches. If you don't want to go in, I could do it for you."

"Thanks, Nikki."

She took off the gloves and washed her hands. "You need a new shirt." She turned and gave them a nod. "I'm going to get one of George's famous steaks."

As she went down the stairs, Gwyn's voice could still be heard. "She doesn't talk much, does she? I don't remember her being such an odd cookie in high school." Not wanting to hear Adrian's reply, she double-timed on the stairs. The food did smell good, even if the company was more than she could bear.

There had to be a corner she could hide out

in while she waited for her sisters. This was not her type of thing anymore. Somewhere along the way, she had become an odd cookie.

"There you are." Danica stood by the stairs. "I was about to come up and find out what was taking so long." She glanced behind Nikki. "Where's Adrian and Gwyn?"

"Apparently he needs help picking out a clean shirt." *Okay, Nikki girl, that sounds like you care.* She shook her head and smiled at her sister. "Those steaks smell so good. I'm starving." Giving Adrian space in her brain had to stop. If Gwyn was interested in him, then more power to her.

Loading down a plate, she talked to several people and seemed to answer the same question one hundred times. Seeking out a quiet dark corner, she ended up outside on the edge of the patio. Settling into the rocking chair, she enjoyed the peace and quiet as she savored the grilled steak and vegetables.

It was so clear, the constellations were easy to spot. Footsteps interrupted her thoughts. Nikki's shoulder slumped a bit. It sounded like one of her sisters. They were probably worried because she was out here by herself. They didn't understand she liked it.

"Hey, why are you out here alone?" Danica

sat down without being invited. "I have extra brownies and cookies."

"Thanks." Nikki had a feeling that would not be the end of it.

"You should be inside. Gwyn's decided that Adrian is all hers."

"I should care because?"

"We've all seen how y'all react to each other."

"I'm not staying. Adrian is the kind of guy that needs a long-term relationship." No point in denying the attraction, but she'd learned the hard way that only took you down the wrong road. "I don't have the time or the energy to play games."

"You could stay. Everything you want can be found in Clear Water, and your family is here. We've missed you. Plus—" she lowered her voice as if someone might overhear "—we think Gwyn is all wrong for Adrian."

With a snort, Nikki gave her sister the look, but it didn't work the way it did back in the day. Danica just sighed. "She didn't even seem to notice him until the pole-bending accident."

Why couldn't her sister let it go? "Women are attracted to men who they see as protectors. It's basic human biology. Of course she is going to pursue him. Any woman would find a man that saved her son attractive. It goes back to our hunting and gathering days."

"What about love? Do you believe we have someone God made for us? A perfect someone that will balance us and love us completely?"

"Oh, I'm pretty sure love is a myth. Trust and respect are the best you can hope for, and I'm not sure I have much faith in those anymore." She looked at her sister. There was a light air of sadness that settled around Danica. "What about the girls' father? Did you love him?"

Danica gave her the saddest smile before she leaned her head back and gazed at the night sky. Silence lingered. Nikki regretted the question. It was easier to avoid personal wounds and scars.

"With every fiber of my being." Rough with emotion, Danica's voice was low. The moonlight reflected off the moisture that had gathered in her eyes. "I brought him home from college, and our father didn't like him. He even told Daddy that he wanted to marry me. I was so happy." She sighed. "Of course, Daddy forbade it. He said I was too young and Reid was just a street kid. Couldn't be trusted."

She crossed her arms and sighed. "At the time, I thought he was just being…you know, a dad. Turned out he was right. Reid was a runner, not a protector. He took off and never came back. I completely trusted him. For the longest time, I thought he would find his way back to me and have an explanation I could forgive. It took me a couple years of convincing my heart that I gave everything to a man who didn't deserve any part of me." Danica reached over and grabbed her hand. "At least you're too smart to let a man take off with your heart. I've always admired how strong and independent you are. You're not afraid of anything."

Nikki squeezed her sister's hand. The pressure in her chest threatened to shatter her into a million pieces. She needed to tell them the truth, but the words were tangled in the logjam in her throat. Her sister that she abandoned was calling her strong.

"There you are!" Jackie stood in the opened door, the light behind her creating a silhouette. "We need to reclaim our title. Come on. The Bible brain game is about to start."

Danica laughed and stood. She pulled Nikki up. "The last four years we've won the Bible trivia challenge. You were always spot-on with your Bible verse competitions. Your room is still full of all the ribbons."

Their mother had been so proud of her memorization ability. Nikki had taken it to heart after her mother died, and wouldn't let anyone beat her.

Danica walked toward Jackie, pulling Nikki along. "Remember how she would beat everyone? Even the older kids. Those couples don't know what is about to hit them. The Bergmann sisters are reunited!"

Nikki had to chuckle. "I'm not sure that's the Christian attitude your pastor would want."

The twins both turned to her with the same look. "Who are you, and where's our sister?"

They had grown into beautiful women while she was running, but for a moment she saw the mischievous girls they were when the world was perfect.

She wanted to hug them close and never let go, but their world did fall apart and time didn't care about broken hearts or dreams. It just kept marching. With a deep sigh, she moved into the restored barn and headed for the group that gathered on the sofas around the fireplace.

It looked as if the teams were ready to go. Five couples sat on one side while the singles gathered on the opposite side of the large coffee table, the game board between them. Katy stood with her arms crossed. "But you got Pastor John when he was single. Why can't we get him now that he's married?"

Everyone started talking. George stood up. "Because you had Coach Calhoune and his wife. They both went to seminary school before becoming teachers, so it was even."

"I'll be the facilitator. Someone needs to be in charge of you guys or it's going to get ugly."

Pastor John winked at her. "Nikki, we haven't met yet. I'm Pastor John Levi." He walked across the open space and held his hand out. "Are you as competitive as your sisters? If so, the couples might be in trouble again this year."

Danica pulled Nikki by the sofa. "I say bring it on! We have the undefeated Bible verse champ with us now. Sit down so we can get this thing started."

Her sister waved to the empty spot next to Adrian. Everyone seemed to be smiling at her, so she made sure not to publicly glare at Danica. But her sister was going to get an earful later. This matchmaking had to stop.

Adrian scooted over a little to give her more room. On the other side of him sat Gwyn. She gave Nikki a friendly smile.

Sitting as close to the edge as she could, Nikki kept her spine stiff. Adrian leaned into her space. "Relax." His breath tickled her ear. "No one will hold it against you if we lose for the first time in four years." He had the nerve to wink at her before he settled back between her and Gwyn.

She knew he had almost kissed her the other day. Now he was acting as if they were best friends. Relax? She'd show him how relaxed she was when it came to winning.

As the questions went back and forth, the

laughter got louder. At one point, Nikki sat back and watched her sisters steal from the married couples with a question about the kings of the Old Testament. Her chest tightened.

It had been too long, so long that she forgot how much she loved being in a group like this. When had she become so isolated and alone?

Pastor John added a point to the single parents' team. "Okay, married couples, you have to get this point to stay in the game. Garrett and Anjelica, what happened at the sixth hour of the crucifixion?" He set the timer.

Garrett looked at his wife. "I have no idea. It would be in Matthew or Luke, right?"

As the timer went off, Anjelica yelled, "Earthquake!"

"Sorry." Pastor John turned to Nikki. "You have a chance to steal the point and, with a two-point lead, win the game." He asked the question again and hit the timer.

Everyone was looking at her. She sat up and gave her audience a slow smile. "At noon or the sixth hour, depending on the version you read, darkness covered the land."

The singles started cheering, but Pastor John lifted his hand. "And a verse."

She closed her eyes and pressed her fingertips to her forehead. She knew this. "Matthew… Matthew…"

Adrian's shoulder bumped hers as he leaned into her. "Matthew 27:45, Mark 15:33 and Luke 23—"

"Now you're just showing off." Katy Buchannan cut him short as she crossed her arms and gave them an exaggerated pout. Everyone laughed, including Adrian.

He held his hand up for a high five. She couldn't stop the smile. It was good to be part of the fun and not just watching it. As a guide, she had got used to watching groups around the campfire laugh and talk all night. She had become accustomed to being on the outside of the circle. Being in the middle felt good.

Vickie put an arm around Katy. "You know, I'm thinking as well as Nikki and Adrian work together, we could have them on our team by next year."

Heat climbed Nikki's neck. Why was everyone trying to put them together to the point of talking marriage? Standing, she looked to the exit. The local state trooper Garrett stood also. He held his hand out to Anjelica and pulled her to his side. "We need to head home. It's past our bedtime."

His new wife patted his chest and laughed. "He's having a harder time with both of us being away from Rio and Pilar than the kids are having being away from us."

Katy and Rhody stood. "Time for us to save the babysitter from our four darling monsters."

Nikki looked at Danica. She hated depending on someone else to get anywhere. Her sister did not look as if she had plans to leave with the couples getting their kids.

Adrian joined her in front of the fireplace. "How are you feeling? You've been on your leg without crutches. Is it hurting?"

"Why would you say that?" She straightened, just in case the pain climbing her spine could be seen in her stance.

"You look as if you want to escape, but don't have a way out." He moved closer and offered her his arm. "How about I escort you to Danica's car and then tell her you're ready and already waiting? It might hurry her up and give you an opportunity to rest out of sight. I also have a question." He started walking, and she followed…again.

Chapter Seven

As they stepped out of the light from the security lamps and deeper into the dark, Nikki leaned heavier into Adrian's support. It was nice to not have to hide her weakness.

"You said you had a question?"

He glanced at the starry sky as if trying to find something he lost. "I thought we made a good team tonight."

It had been a long time since she felt like she belonged anywhere, let alone on a team. Adrian was one of the true good guys. With his profile to her, she could study his features. Still good-looking, the years added maturity and depth. She didn't really understand why he was still single.

He put his hands in the front pockets of his worn-just-right jeans. With a quick turn of his head, he looked at her before going back to the sky. "Anyway, I was wondering if you liked live music." He looked down. "Mia is going to her first sleepover since the accident, and George has some sort of plans out of town." He took a deep breath. "So would you want to go to Kerrville with me? A friend from the bull-riding days is playing at a restaurant, and I thought going there would be better than sitting alone and worrying about Mia, but I don't want to go alone."

She waited for him to finish. After a moment of silence, it seemed he was done talking. "Are you asking me on a date?"

"No! Yes. Which would be better?" He shook his head. "Since I'm asking you to go to dinner with me, and there's music, it'd be like a date. But if you don't want to call it a date, we could invite your sisters."

She couldn't hold back a laugh. This might be why he wasn't married yet. She found it irresistible. "That might be the worst line I've ever heard."

A lopsided grin reminded her of the boy she knew back in school.

"Sorry. That was pretty lame." He turned to her, searching her face. His dark eyes so intense, she had to look away. Heat crawled up her neck.

"I'm a bit rusty, and dating anyone in town has been a hassle. Whenever I did try to go out, everyone started asking about a date for the wedding."

She raised one eyebrow. Had he not heard the suggestions of them getting married before the next mixed social? "We haven't even been on a date, and they're already planning the colors for our wedding."

He chuckled. "Yeah, I heard the hints about us making a good couple, but those don't count because you'll be leaving and everyone knows that."

"This only reminds me of why I left. The small-town attitude that everyone has a right to know your business and give unsolicited advice is a beat down. How have you done it for so long?"

He shrugged. "They're not that bad."

At her look of disbelief, he laughed.

"Really, they've been there when I needed them. Being a single teen dad was not easy, but they made it possible. They really do have our best interest at heart. I've learned to ignore it for the most part. You have to take the good with the bad, you know."

"You're a better person than me."

He reached behind her to open the back door. "Let's get you off your leg and settled into the car. And forget about my question. I'd like to—"

"Adrian!" Gwyn hurried over to them. "My

car won't start. I'm not sure what it is, but I might need a jump. Could you help me?"

He glanced over his shoulder. Danica and Jackie were right behind Gwyn.

Jackie turned to Gwyn. "Nikki's great with cars. Maybe she could help you."

"Nikki needs to get off her feet." He shot her sisters a warning glare. "I know she won't admit it. But she is still recovering from major reconstructive surgery." Adrian turned to her and assisted her into the car. She buried the instinctive response to deny his claim and his help. Over the years, going to the rescue was her job, even before the navy, when her sisters were little and without a mother.

Settling into the back seat, she gave him a smile. He leaned in and, for a moment, she thought he was going to kiss her. The clean leather smell of his skin made her okay with that. She closed her eyes. The solid click of her seat belt pulled her out of that stupid fantasy. He was helping her, making sure she was safe. Just like he did with everyone else, including Gwyn.

The doors opened and the twins got in the front seats. "Thanks, Adrian."

"Sure—anytime. Y'all be safe." With a wave, he turned to fix Gwyn's problems.

Danica put the SUV in Reverse. "I can't believe Gwyn did that. We hung back to give you time alone with Adrian and she had to find a way to interrupt."

Jackie twisted in her seat to look at Nikki. "Did he ask you out?"

Thrusting her head back against the headrest, Nikki looked at some kind of juice stain on the roof. "Why would you even go there?"

Steering onto the road, Danica clicked her tongue. "You were getting along so well, and everyone saw what a great team you made. At times you actually finished—"

"Each other's sentences." The twins erupted into laughter. It was hard to stay mad when laughter filled the space. Man, she had missed them, even if they did want to meddle in her life.

"I wouldn't be surprised if she left her lights on just so she could ask Adrian for help."

"Who would even think of doing that?" Nikki couldn't imagine someone being that needy. "Playing the little helpless woman sounds stupid to me."

"Hey, don't knock it." Danica made eye contact in the rearview mirror. "It's a safe way to talk to a guy you're interested in without being too forward."

Jackie nearly jumped out of her seat belt. "Danica Elizabeth Bergmann! You did that when and with who? Did it work? Do I know him?"

Silence followed the whirlwind of questions.

About the time Nikki thought she wasn't going to answer, Dani cleared her throat.

"You've met him. Nikki hasn't. Forget I said anything."

Jackie gasped then laid a hand on her twin's arm. "Reid?" She looked at Nikki. "Reid McAllister. He's the twins'—"

"I don't want to talk about him." Her knuckles were tight around the steering wheel, and her jaw was set as she stared down the road.

"Okay. We were talking about Adrian and Nikki anyway."

With a groan, Nikki closed her eyes. Was she really just thinking how much she missed her sisters? "What about you, Jackie? Any guys in your life?"

"Come on, Nikki. You and Adrian would make a great couple."

"First of all, I'm not staying, and I can guarantee he is not a casual-dater kind of guy. Second, I think he did ask me out, but it was so awkward I'm not really sure. And third, he's younger than me."

"By three measly years. Wait, he did ask you?"

"What do you mean awkward? Like how?"

She lifted her leg to stretch it out along the back seat. "He invited you both to come along. My knee is hurting. I need to put ice on it as soon as we get home. Jackie, are we dropping you off at your house or you staying the night again?"

"Oh, no you don't. You could care less about your knee, so don't start using it now."

She blew out a puff of air, forcing stray strands of hair out of her eyes. They were going to make her talk. "He started with Mia having a sleepover, and how he worries too much. Then he said he has a friend playing in a band and wondered if I liked live music."

"He invited us? That's bad. What did you say?" Danica turned on her blinker.

"Gwyn came up with her car problems and that was it."

"He did ask you out though. How cute." Jackie hit her twin's shoulder.

Danica laughed. "I think I was the last date he had, and that was four years ago. It was a disaster. He had to be nervous."

"And you don't find me going out with him a bit uncomfortable?" Nikki couldn't believe she was even contemplating going on a date with a guy that took her sister out.

"Oh no. We're friends and help each other out as single parents. He's involved with the 4-H Club, the church youth program and a mentor with the teen-parent program in Uvalde. He's a great guy." She shrugged. "It just didn't click between us. You know?" Her gaze cut to the rearview mirror. "Right now in my life, I need to focus on the girls. At the time, I still had Reid in my head. You need to date a nice guy and get over the last jerk."

Jackie turned again. "Adrian is really the best. Maybe he's always liked you. A lot of the guys liked you in high school, but you weren't interested in anyone."

No, she had been all into a guy who was using her. She allowed him to treat her like a dirty secret. "Maybe he's too nice. I'm a train wreck."

Danica snorted as she pulled into the long drive to the family home where they grew up. "You can't have done anything worse than me. I mean, come on. I went off to college and came home alone with twins." She jammed the beast into Park. They all sat there in the dark. Jackie removed her seat belt and wrapped Danica in her arms.

"And now we have two more beautiful girls in our family. Which is good because I don't think I'm ever having kids, and at the rate Nikki is going, she'll never make me an aunt. She has her life all together and doesn't need a man."

Her stomach flopped and punched. Pressing her hands tightly against her middle didn't help. If she didn't say something now, she probably never would. It wasn't fair that they didn't know the truth. "Danica, I'm so proud of you and how you handled the situation. I've done worse, but I ran and hid from everyone."

The twins looked at her. They both reached across the seat and held out their hands until Nikki joined them and formed their triangle. Jackie smiled. "The Triad. Remember you started this when we were little and said we would always have each other no matter what? It's for you too, big sister."

She nodded. There was no gentle way to start this, so she jumped in with both feet. "Back in high school? I didn't leave my senior year because of Dad's ex-wife." She heard the bitterness in her own voice. Filling her lungs to capacity, she held her breath before forcing it all out. "It was easy to blame it on Sheila because we were fighting all the time, but I..." Each of the twins squeezed their hands around her wrist. The words lodged in her throat, threatening her ability to breathe. It was just mental. She could do this. "I was pregnant, and I didn't want Daddy to know."

Lifting her chin, she looked up. Danica and Jackie looked at her as if she had spoken another language. After what seemed like an eternity of silence, both girls jumped out of the car at the same time. The warmth of their touch vanished. That was it. They were gone.

Before another thought could form, they had the back doors open and were scrambling inside to hold her like they would never let her go. Her eyes burned and her vision blurred. She blinked a couple of times before admitting she had tears trying to escape. They had her arms pinned and she couldn't wipe the senseless things away.

Danica leaned back and used her thumb to clear the wet trail off Nikki's cheek. "What happened to the baby?"

"Our great-aunt Gloria became my legal guardian and helped set up an adoption. Her grandson and his wife wanted to adopt, but they were on a waiting list so long they had given up. When she went to them, they were so excited and the baby was actually family, so that was a good thing. It was a little boy. They named him Parker."

"So it was an open adoption? Why didn't you tell us?"

"I still don't understand why you left. Who's the father?" They spoke so fast and on top of each other she wasn't sure who said what.

"I was the strong one, the one who held the family together when Momma died. I didn't think Daddy could handle it along with all of Sheila's drama. I just...ran. I couldn't face him, couldn't see the hurt and disappointment in his eyes." She swallowed down the acid that threatened to spill over. She was in this far. She might as well tell them everything. "Tommy Miller."

In unison the twins gasped. "Did he...?"

"No. No, it was nothing like that. I was in love and he told me that Vickie didn't really love him, but their parents were pushing them together. He needed Mr. Lawson's recommendation to get into law school and the scholarships he wanted. He said if I could just wait, that once we left for college it would be just the two of us. He told me I kept him sane, and I believed every word." Head down, she squeezed her eyes shut. How could she have been so stupid not to see he had used her? She had been his dark secret.

"Hey. What's going on out here?" All three jumped at Sammi's voice. Their little sister stood just outside the door behind Jackie. "Everything okay? Are y'all crying?" She moved in closer, but then backed up. "I'm sorry. I didn't mean to interrupt."

"Oh no, it's fine." Nikki reached past Jackie and held her hand out. Her baby sister wasn't a baby anymore. A grown woman stood in front of her. "We're having a sister talk and you should be here."

Jackie twisted to make room for Sammi in the tight space.

Sammi wrapped her arms around her middle. "So what are you talking about?"

Danica and Jackie both looked at Nikki. She didn't have another word left in her.

Clearing her throat, Jackie started backing out the Suburban. "We should continue in the house. I'm too old to be hiding in the back seat."

Sammi followed. "But why are you all crying?"

The twins exchanged a look then turned to Nikki. With a quick nod, she gave them permission to tell their little sister. Danica started the story and Jackie finished.

Sammi stopped. "That's why you left us, Nikki? Y'all knew?"

Danica put her arm around Sammi, but she pulled away. "No. No one knew."

Glancing among them all, Jackie looked to Nikki for help. "We just now found out."

The hurt in Sammi's eyes gave Nikki another reason to feel guilty. She wanted to hug her, but the don't-come-close look warned her to keep her distance. "So cousins on your mom's side have him?"

Nikki managed a nod and stepped forward, hand reaching for Sammi.

Her baby sister took a step back. "Daddy blamed Momma for you leaving." Sam bit her bottom lip and looked toward the house before leveling a stare at Nikki again. "So it wasn't my mother's fault?"

"No, she's not the reason I left. I'm so sorry." There wasn't anything left to say.

"We have to tell Daddy. He has always blamed Momma."

Nikki nodded. With a sigh, she put an arm around Sammi and held on tight this time. She wasn't going to lose her baby sister. "I'm sorry. You're right. I need to tell him."

Tears in her eyes, Sammi nodded.

The twins wrapped their arms around them. She found herself in the middle of a warm hug from all three sisters. *God, please forgive me for not having enough faith to be honest about my mistakes.*

This was why she needed to stay away from Adrian and the temptation of wanting what she couldn't afford to risk. Once she told her father, she was sure he would want her to leave. All the years he had blamed Sheila because of her mistake… Would he forgive her?

Her sisters surrounded her in love, but she couldn't see their stubborn and stern father letting go of the past so easily.

The front porch light came on. "What are y'all doing out there in the dark? Girls, get in the house."

With her sisters walking by her side, she passed through the front door of her childhood home. She needed to keep her focus on her plan.

Get better and get the funds to buy her own business. A business to fill her days with adventures of the physical kind, far from Clear Water and Adrian De La Cruz. He was dangerous to her heart.

Chapter Eight

Adrian took the smoothed wood from George. He glanced over at Nikki. She'd barely said hi when he walked into the store this morning. Now she seemed to be avoiding him by organizing the old chairs, separating the broken ones from the solid ones. Her whole body moved as she sanded the top of a huge abandoned pine table.

Did he ask her out again or just wait for her to say something? Normally he would talk to George, but he hesitated, which worried him also. The song "I Just Can't Wait to Be King" sounded from his brother's front shirt pocket. Nikki looked at them with a raised eyebrow. He had to laugh as his brother's dark skin turned red. Should he save his brother's man card and explain the fairy-tale song? George stepped into the staircase.

The new polished wood warmed Adrian's hands as he lined it up. Now would be a good time to ask. He leaned the plank against the exposed rock and turned to face her.

His twin came up the steps. "That was Mrs. Miller, again. She says we left some tools in the sheep barn. I know we didn't. Those are her husband's old tools."

Adrian shook his head. "Go. She probably just needs someone to talk to. I can finish this. After lunch we can start taking down the old drywall in the rest of the rooms."

"Sure you're not just looking to get rid of me?" Eyebrows wiggled followed by laughter that had Adrian gritting his teeth. "And you need to teach your daughter about the privacy of people's belongings." George waved his phone.

If Adrian had anything with some weight, he'd throw it at his brother's retreating back. She could think whatever she wanted about his brother. He wasn't going to explain the cartoon ringtone.

With his twin gone, he joined Nikki at the table she rubbed down. He ran his hand along the grain she had already polished. The wood glowed with new life, but a few stains and flaws still remained. He liked the evidence of all the people who had used the table in the past, bits of stories embedded into the wood. Nikki kept her attention on her work. She acted as if he wasn't in the room, let alone standing next to her.

"George's ringtone was Mia's doing." His twin owed him. "She gets a kick out of messing with our settings since I won't let her have a phone of her own. It's her little revenge against us."

She chuckled. "I like your daughter. It did surprise me. I always thought of George as more of a classic guy, Patsy Cline and Hank Williams."

"Speaking of music. Last night I asked if you wanted to have dinner with me."

She looked up at him and smiled. That had to be a good sign. He leaned a hip on the edge of the table and crossed his arms. "Well, I kind of asked. So now I'm asking you on a real date. You know, the kind grown-ups do. Just you and me. No sisters, brothers or daughters." He watched her face, but she kept her head down, focused on the table. "I'd think we'd have fun together."

"As long as you know I'm leaving. Once I'm one hundred percent and have enough money saved up, I'm going back to Arizona."

"So it's a date. Next Thursday?"

"Why not?" She shrugged and looked up at him with a slight grin before going back to the old table.

Not a huge endorsement. He wanted her to look at him again. "What's the money for?"

"Money?" She was looking at him, but confusion marked her eyes.

"You said you were here to save some money. I was wondering what you were saving for."

"Oh." And back to the table her attention went. "I want to start my own outfitters company, wild adventure tours. How long have you and George run your own business?"

Before he could answer, a tentative knock warned them that they were not alone. Adrian looked up and blinked a couple of times. There was no way he was seeing this correctly. Charlotte Walker stood in the open door frame. Her hair was lighter, but it was the person who'd walked out on him and his daughter over ten years ago.

Numbness gave way to a sudden pulse of blood driving through his veins. What was she doing here?

"Hi, Adrian. It's me, Charlotte."

"I know who you are. What I don't know is why you're here."

From the edge of his vision he saw Nikki stand. "Hello, Charlotte." She held her hand out. "I'm Nikki Bergmann."

Charlotte gave her a tight smile while shaking her hand. "I remember you. Your sister told me

Adrian was up here. I'm sorry to barge in like this, but I need to talk to Adrian, and I thought this would be a safe place."

"Sure." She turned to Adrian. "I'll go downstairs for a bit. Let me know when you want to get back to work."

"Stay." His gaze stayed on Mia's mother. "I'll be back to work soon enough, and I'd rather not be alone." He forced his hands to relax from the knotted fists they had made when she walked into the room. Flexing his fingers, he looked at Nikki. "Stay, please."

"Okay." She moved to stand behind the table.

"Why are you here?" *Breathe, breathe.*

"I recently finished college and have a nursing job in Kerrville. I even have my own place. I, um… I've been sober for three years now." She pulled a coin out of her pocket and showed it to him as if it proved something.

His stomach turned. "You're living in Kerrville?" That was too close.

She nodded with quick jerks, looking a little desperate. "Yeah, I finally have my life together."

"Great, but I still don't know why you're here, at my place of work." In his gut he was afraid he did know. Mia. She wanted Mia.

"I've been working with a therapist, and we agree that I'm ready to meet my daughter."

"She's not your daughter anymore. You gave up all rights and walked out on us. You haven't called or written. Nothing for ten years. Now you want to meet her? You didn't even want to hold her on the day she was born, the day you gave birth to her."

"I wasn't ready, and I knew if I looked at her I wouldn't be able to let her go. I had to leave. I'm sorry, but I did what I thought was best for all of us at the time."

Rage that he thought he'd got over ten years ago boiled from the pit of his stomach, nearly choking him. "I gave up everything and all you gave up was my daughter. It's too late. We don't need you now."

Hand out, she stepped closer to him. "I know I hurt you and I'm sorry, but I was too selfish to be a mother. I was also alone. I didn't have the kind of support that surrounded you. My dad was a raging alcoholic. My mom only wanted to keep him happy. I couldn't count on them for support. You had your mom, dad and George, not to mention your sisters. They hated me." She looked down, dropping her hand.

He just stood there, letting the silence hang between them. She started twisting her hands, acting scared.

She had the nerve to lie then act as if he was

being too hard on her. "Don't you dare play the victim here." The blood pounded in his ears.

He needed to settle down and get her out of here, but it was like all the anger he had pushed down now had the opportunity to lash out and say all the things he had wanted to say to her ten years ago, but she had left without a word. Just a note and the note was long gone, ripped to shreds.

"Now you're making stuff up. They didn't hate you. But none of that matters. You need to leave. Mia doesn't need a mother. You decided that when you left us."

Her gaze darted to Nikki then back to him. "You had the whole town. I was an outsider who dared to ruin the local star's future. I didn't have what you had. Adrian, I didn't have anyone."

"You had me." His fist slammed into his chest. "My family was more than willing to take you in and help with the baby. You didn't want our help." He stood closer and pointed a finger at her. "You just wanted the next party."

She pulled her light sweater tight around her chest. "Yes, my priorities were a mess. It was not me they were helping. It was you and our daughter."

"You were her mother. That made you family. So don't act like we pushed you out."

Lowering her head, Charlotte rubbed her temple. "I'm not." She looked back at him. "Adrian, you don't understand what it's like to be alone in the world, where everything is temporary, even your parents' affection. I couldn't comprehend your family and their unconditional love. I didn't see how I'd fit into that circle. I was an outsider. That was all I knew." She wiped at a few tears that managed to spill over. "I didn't come here to fight or make excuses. I did mess up. I'm not here to claim myself as her mother. I know I deserve your anger."

He wasn't moved.

She held an envelope out for him. He didn't blink. His hard gaze stayed on her. His hands clinched at his sides as he stared her down, not making a move to take the letter.

With a sigh, she finally looked down. A trembling hand laid the light blue envelope on the table edge. "I know I don't deserve her forgiveness, but I tried to explain what I was going through as a seventeen-year-old and why I thought the best thing for everyone was to leave her with you. I knew you would provide a safe home and love that I couldn't give. I just want the chance to meet her. I thought she might want to meet her mother."

"For ten years I've been her only parent. I protected her, and loved her, and watched her grow. You are the woman that gave birth to her.

Then walked away. That's all. Why would she want to talk to you?"

"I know I don't deserve to just waltz back into her life. That's why I came to you first. I understand, and you have every right to be angry at me. All I'm asking is that you share the letter with her and talk about it. If she has no desire to see me, then that's fine. I won't make contact again. The letter is unsealed so you can read it first. My personal information, work numbers and my doctor's information is in the letter if you want to talk to them first. I won't be back unless you call me."

Ugly words screamed for release in his head, but he locked his jaw tight and glared at her. He knew he was reacting like a hotheaded teenage boy, but he couldn't lock the rage back in its box. She gave him a tentative smile and nodded to Nikki before turning her back to him and disappearing down the stairs.

His nostrils flared with hard breaths. Stomping to the back room, he grabbed the edge of the broken and decaying Sheetrock and yanked with every burning muscle in his body, ripping the dilapidated walls from the raw stone.

The rage he had bottled for ten years pulsed through his veins. He had given up his senior year to be a father. He had walked away from his dream of being a professional bull rider, of traveling. She hadn't even stayed long enough to see their tiny baby girl home.

Now she walked in with a letter and wanted back into their lives. He reached for the next sheet of drywall and found nothing but exposed limestone. He slammed the rock wall hard, and pain shot through his arms. He turned and looked around the room.

Chunks of broken drywall cluttered the floor. He stood in the midst of destruction. Leaning forward, he pressed his palms to his thighs and tried to get his breathing under control. Counting the hard puffs, he tried to focus.

God, I don't know what You want from me. He looked at the shambles of the old wall. The level of his anger scared him. He heard a noise and turned to the open door. Nikki stood there. Had she been watching the whole time? Had she seen him lose control?

Nikki wasn't sure what to say or if she should have even stayed. He was hurt and probably wanted to be alone, but she was worried he would accidentally hurt himself.

"Well, Mr. Hulk, you got that job done faster than you had said it would take."

He looked down, his ribs still expanding hard and heavy. "I didn't damage anything we weren't taking down."

"I know. Are you okay? Do you need to talk about it?" Ugh. Did she really suggest he should talk? She hated it when people talked about emotion.

His stare made her feel like a fraud. "Would you let her back in your life?"

"You just got blindsided from the past. I know how difficult that could be, and you got the old walls down in record time without George. I say you don't pay him."

He gave her a sad grin that pulled at her stupid heart. "Sounds good to me. But then maybe I'll pay him extra for cleaning up my mess. He's done it before." His gaze swept the room. "What do you think about giving the letter to Mia?"

He wasn't going to let her change the subject. "My concern would be someone sees Charlotte and tells your daughter that her mother was in town. Hearing that from someone else wouldn't be good."

He growled and threw his fist against the rough stone again. He pulled his phone from his shirt pocket, shaking the hand that now had bloody knuckles. He looked at the screen, and his jaw clenched. He said something under his breath. Not a good sign. "What is it?"

Adrian tilted his head back and pinched the

bridge of his nose. "George, my mother and both of my sisters have been calling. I'm thinking the gossips have already been to work." He hit the screen and put the phone to his ear. "George—" Eyes closed, he shook his head. "Yes, she was here. She gave me a letter for Mia and wants to see her."

Nikki grabbed a clean rag and poured some of her water over it. Without asking permission, she started cleaning his hand. She needed something to do.

He looked at Nikki, the kind of look that went past her walls. She wanted to run, but she planted her feet and focused on the damaged hand.

"Did Mom tell her anything?" he asked his brother.

He pulled his hand free from her. Stepping over the debris, Adrian moved into the other room. He stopped at the table and sighed. "I'll meet you at Mom and Dad's for lunch." Slipping the phone back into his pocket, he looked at the light blue envelope. Something needed to be said, some sort of words strung together to offer encouragement, but she sucked at emotional hoopla.

"So word is already out?" She stood next to him. "Seventeen-year-old girls make mistakes.

You said you relied on your faith to get you through. Would that include forgiving her?" Nikki felt as if her own heart was asking for forgiveness.

Adrian took his stare off the unread letter and looked at her. "Right now I'm not sure I'm on good enough terms with God to forgive her." He started to reach for the letter, but instead made a sharp turn away from it.

Burying his fingers in his thick hair, he braced himself against the new window frame and looked down into the street. "Thank you for tending my hand. That was an immature move on my part." He looked at the back of his injured hand and flexed his fingers. "What I don't get was how she could carry Mia for that whole time then turn her back on us. On her daughter."

He looked at Nikki. The need for answers burned in his eyes. All she could do was shrug. "In her mind, she wasn't abandoning her baby. She left her with you and your family. Would you have wanted her to be around Mia with the problems she was struggling with at the time?"

"And how do I know she's better? Maybe she still shouldn't be around Mia."

Nikki tried to swallow past the dry clogged mess in her throat. There was no way she could go out with him if he couldn't forgive Charlotte for leaving their daughter with him. "Open the letter. Contact the people she listed. The doctor, her boss… They have no reason to lie." She picked up the envelope and walked over to him, holding it out.

His gaze searched hers. Her lungs started burning. She forgot to breathe. She didn't want to examine the reason his forgiveness for Charlotte mattered so much to her.

He finally took the envelope. "I guess I don't really have a choice now. She's here and Mia will know as soon as she goes to town." He pulled one of the old chairs up to the table and planted his elbows on the edge. He dropped the letter and rubbed his forehead.

"What kind of woman leaves her child after giving birth? I don't want her around my daughter." With a heavy sigh, he ripped open the envelope. His hand flexed as if he wanted to tear it to shreds. He dropped it and looked up at Nikki. "Her handwriting looks exactly the same on the letter she left at the hospital. I thought I had put this anger behind me. Maybe you can read it out loud?"

Nikki brought a chair over and sat across from him. Tommy hadn't given her a letter. He just told her to get rid of "it," and he'd deny it was his if she said anything. Tommy *had* abandoned his child in every way. Charlotte had left her baby in good hands with someone who she knew would love her and give her a safe home. Would Adrian be able to see that?

"Dear Mia,
I'm not sure what your father has told you, and I'm not sure how to introduce myself. I'm Charlotte Walker. I gave birth to you, and unfortunately was not able to stay and help raise you. It had nothing to do with you. You were perfect. Your father was holding you the first time I saw you. His parents, your grandparents, and his brother were surrounding him. They all wanted to hold the new baby, but he wouldn't give you up. Till this day, I've never seen such love on someone's face."

A drop of water fell onto the paper, causing the ink to bleed a little. Nikki looked up and then realized it was a tear, from her. She wiped the back of her hand across her eyes. She glanced at Adrian to see his reaction and was about to apologize, but his head was down. With his elbows planted on his knees, he was staring at the floor.

When he looked up at her, a frown creased his forehead. "Is that it? She ended it there?" He looked confused.

"No." She took a deep breath. "This is very personal. Are you sure you want me to read it?"

Adrian moved his elbows back to the table, covered his left hand with his right and rested his mouth against them. His eyes closed and he gave a nod, encouraging her to keep going. She wasn't sure she could. One deep breath, and then she started reading again.

"Mia, I was so messed up. My parents were toxic. So different from the De La Cruz family. I knew your father would love you and provide a safe place to grow up, surrounded by people who would show you how a real family supported and loved each other. I made the decision right there to leave. Maybe a part of me was running in fear of being a mother, but the other part of me was afraid of bringing the poison of my parents into your life. I might be telling you too much, but I was still battling drugs and alcohol. I didn't have God in my life. Once I found out about you, your father pretty much stayed with me, making sure I stayed clean. I was never sure what he saw in me anyway. He has a very big heart.

My first thought when I gave birth to you was now I could have a drink. That should not have been my desire, and I knew I was being controlled by it. I was so afraid of hurting you, of disappointing Adrian. You were so beautiful and tiny. I didn't want my drama to contaminate your world, so I left. It took a while for me to figure things out. I finally turned my life over to God.

It has not been easy, but I have been clean for three years now. I have a good job in Kerrville and thought it was time to reach out to you. If you are reading this, then your father has allowed me to be a part of your life. It is up to you. I know I gave up any rights when I left. If you want to talk or meet, your father will get in contact with me. I will be waiting for however long you need."

Carefully, Nikki folded the letter and put it back in the envelope. She slid the letter across the table and left it for Adrian. "What are you going to do?"

"She set this up so I would have to tell Mia."

"What do you mean?"

"She could have mailed it, or called me first." He stood and walked to the window, running his hand through his now-messy hair. "Instead she made it very public by walking right into the hardware store where everyone in town would see her. There's no way I'd be able to keep this from my daughter. As soon as Mia steps foot in town, someone will tell her that her mother was here, talking to me. She forced my hand. I don't have a real choice but to give the letter to Mia."

"What are you afraid will happen? The other night you talked about trusting God. Do you trust Him?"

"But what if He gave her to me, trusting that I'll protect her? I failed once already, and she has screws and rods in her leg. Now she's mad at me for keeping her from the horses." He sat back down and looked at her. "I do trust God, but that doesn't mean I don't have responsibilities as her father. My job is to keep the people that will hurt her out of her life."

"If Charlotte has cleaned up her life, then how will it hurt?"

"She walked out on us once already. Do you know how devastating that was to me? My gut says to keep Charlotte as far from Mia as possible."

"That's not your gut. That's your scars she left when she walked out on *you*. It was devastating to you, yes. But Mia grew up surrounded by love. You, George, your parents and sisters have always been there for her. From what I've seen, she has a whole town that's given her nothing but love and support. She doesn't have your memories or the scars that go with them."

"I don't want her to have my scars." He lifted his head and looked her straight in the eyes. His dark gaze burning into her own guilt.

Nikki's nerves demanded she get up. She wanted to run, but where would she go? What she really wanted was to run from her own past. She needed a cliff to jump off, or a river to battle, but her past was still there, waiting to be dealt with. This was too hard.

Expanding her lungs, she got up and leaned against the door frame. Hands behind her back, she anchored herself by pressing her palms against the warm wood.

Adrian's gaze went back to the large window. "How do I stop her from getting hurt?"

"Be honest with her." She glanced up. *Yes, God, I realize what I'm saying.* "From what I've seen, you've raised a smart and strong-minded little girl." Pushing away from the wall, she took a step closer to Adrian. "You know one of the things I remember about you in school?" Sitting in the chair at the corner of the table, she stopped short of reaching for his hand.

His fingertips tapped the wood she had been sanding down. "You knew what you wanted, and you went after it with a fierce determination. Look at the way you tackled fatherhood. You put your dreams aside and went in all the way. You started your own business from nothing. You found a way to get horses back in your life. You made all that happen. And your daughter? She's just like you."

He gave her a lopsided grin. "You make me sound heroic. I was just following the path God put in front of me." He played at the corner of the envelope.

"You can't control everything in your daughter's life, but you can control how you handle it. Don't give her a reason to resent you. Talk to her with an open mind. Tell her how you feel without making it about your anger." Nikki shrugged. "If given a choice, she might not even want to meet her mother."

"Don't call her that." He lowered his head. "Sorry. I need to get rid of this anger. I know it puts me in a bad place, but how do I let go of her walking out on us?"

"If Mia finds out you tried to keep this from her, that could be a scar you put on her heart. You say you trust God. You have to trust Him with your daughter too."

He snorted and looked at her with a small spark of humor in his eyes. "That's not what I want to hear."

"Opening up and being honest isn't easy. I know. I also know the truth never goes away, no matter how deep you bury it. It darkens all your joy and contaminates your whole life."

He tilted his head. "It sounds like you need to talk." Reaching out, he covered her fidgeting hands. His fingers were warm and slightly rough from working his whole life. "You seem to have it together. What's going on with you?"

"I'm fine. Recently I've realized trying not to deal with something doesn't make it go away. It just silently festers. You need to talk with your daughter. She loves you so much, and I know her loyalty is all yours."

He leaned back and studied her. "You think I might be worried that I will lose Mia to Charlotte?" He looked more relaxed than earlier.

"I think your daughter has never been upset with you until recently, when you forbade her to get back on a horse. You've had her all to yourself for ten years. I don't think you like to share."

He actually tilted his head back and laughed. A low rumbling sound deep in his chest. She could listen to that all day. "You might be right on that score. I hate uncertainty. When Charlotte left, I put her out of my thoughts and moved forward with my daughter." He stood again and ran his hand along the window frame he had been finishing. "I hate the idea that she thinks she can just walk back into my life, say *I'm sorry* and become Mia's mother. I'm her parent, the only one she's needed for ten years."

"Mia's a smart girl. She loves you. She'll make the right choice."

Rubbing the back of his hand, he looked down. "Why were you gone so long?"

The change of subject with a personal question knocked her back a bit. "What?"

"I understand why you left, but why stay gone so long? I thought you were tight with your father and sisters." He leaned closer to her. "Why did you stay away for over ten years? Was it something your father did, or your stepmother?"

She didn't have a problem talking about him and his daughter, but where did she begin even explaining the complicated mess she had created all on her own? A mess she had been too cowardly to face.

Tilting her head back, she studied the white paint chipping and peeling from the designs in the pressed tin. "For a long time, I blamed my father because he was a hard man to talk to. He was stern and kept his emotions out of sight. I knew he loved me, but I couldn't talk to him about mistakes and...well, he was hard to talk to." Shifting her gaze to Adrian, she found him studying her as if trying to see past the facade she used to protect herself.

"I would dare to say you might be the same way." He softened the hard hit with his beautiful grin.

She nodded. "Yes, I remember Momma laughing and teasing my dad that I was just like him, so he didn't have room to get mad at me." She looked directly at Adrian. "You have to keep an open door with Mia. Don't start hiding things thinking you're protecting her. She knows something's wrong and it can start creating a wall between you." She pulled on her bottom lip. "Then when she really needs you, there will be a chasm she thinks she can never cross."

He nodded and leaned back, draping an arm over the back of the chair. "You know I mentor teen parents. I tell them all the time that once you start hiding from the truth, life gets more complicated. It's harder to live by that advice than to give it."

"Now, that's one hundred percent truth." While Adrian scanned the room, Nikki took the opportunity to study him. He looked relaxed. The easygoing mannerisms he showed the world hid the complexity that drove him to be a better dad and man.

The kind of man that might make it worth staying in Clear Water. She shook her head and stood up, needing to move and clear her thoughts. The kind of thoughts that would only get her hurt. Who was she kidding? After his reaction to Charlotte, how would he feel about a woman who gave her baby away?

"You okay?" Concern softened his deep brown eyes.

She turned her back to him. "Yeah. Restless. We've been up here sitting too long. I need to move." Away from him and the fantasy that he could ever want a romantic relationship with her. She suspected if asked, he had her firmly in the friend camp. That made her safe to talk to. Safe to take to dinner.

He touched her arm. "How's your knee? Would you be able to explore the ranch?"

She shook her head. "I promised to stay away from any off-road trips on my bike. I'd have to get a new bike anyway, and there's that money issue."

He laughed. "Do I look like I ride a bicycle?" He glanced down at his jeans and worn cowboy boots. "You want to get out, and our music date isn't until Thursday. I was thinking you could take it slow on a horse. Tomorrow, after church, my sister is taking Mia into Kerrville for a girls' afternoon and I was gonna put some mileage on our two-year-olds. You could visit Swift and we could go riding. If we keep it at a walk, your knee should be fine. We'll stay off the rocky side of the hills. It'll be some safe PT."

She snorted. "That sounds nice. I would love to explore my mom's ranch. I didn't get far before the rain and the deer. Then the fall. Not my finest moment." One of the most humiliating moments in her life. "How is she doing? The fawn. Swift, right?"

"Growing and getting into trouble. Like any healthy kid." He stood and walked past her, stopping at the doorway to the back room. Fists planted on his hips, he shook his head. "I can't believe I had that much anger in me."

"Ten years is a long time to keep it buried."

"This can't be healthy. I'm so sorry. I've never thrown this kind of fit before, even when she left. I've kept it together. Did I scare you?"

"No. I just wasn't sure what to do. I didn't want to leave you alone, but I didn't want to intrude either."

"Thanks for staying." He rubbed the back of his neck. "I guess it's time to head over to Mom's." He looked over his shoulder. "I'll take the letter and give it to Mia." He just stood there looking back at the table, but not making a move to get the letter.

Nikki picked it up and handed it to him. As he took the note from her, sparks ran up her arm and straight to her gut. For a moment, they made eye contact. Her breath froze. With a jerk, she brought her hand back to her side and rubbed it against her jeans. It was just a touch. He still maintained eye contact. "You sure you're okay?"

She nodded. Sadness squeezed her heart. Because of her mistakes, she would never be the kind of woman Adrian could love. Every nerve in her body told her he was the kind of man that once he loved you, he loved you for a million years. Then a million more. "I'm good. I think I might be getting tired."

He reached out and, with a gentle touch, held her upper arm. "Do you need help?"

"No, no." She stepped back and made sure to smile at him. "You have a daughter to talk to. You can't let the sun go down on this. You have to deal with it head-on, like you deal with everything else."

He nodded and looked away. "I might have a harder time with my family than Mia." He sighed and tucked the letter into his front shirt pocket. "You would think I'd know by now that the only certainty in life is the unpredictable. Will you pray for us?"

"I will. Even for Charlotte. I know you'll do what's best for your daughter."

He chuckled. "It's hard being the adult."

"I wouldn't know." She winked at him. Her heart needed some space. She couldn't afford to be falling in love with Adrian De La Cruz.

"I guess I'll see you at church tomorrow. Remember to bring a change of clothes and we'll head straight to the ranch."

"Okay." Church. She was going to church then riding with Adrian. Why had she agreed to that? Because she was going stir-crazy sitting around, but she wasn't allowed to go exploring on her own. She could be friends with Adrian while she was in Clear Water. She was a grown woman.

He disappeared down the side stairs. All the blood left her body, and she collapsed into the closest chair. Dropping her head into her hands, she prayed. She prayed for Mia, Adrian, all of his family and Charlotte. Then she prayed for herself. Tears started falling.

Witnessing all of Adrian's anger turn physical made her realize how much she had been carrying in her heart. She slipped to the floor, and her hurt knee protested as she asked for forgiveness. For the first time in a decade, she turned everything over to God.

A warm touch caused her to jump. Adrian had come back and found her like this. Pushing her hair out of her face, she looked up and found her father. Pulling her up from the floor, he cupped her face.

"Nicole? Please tell me what's wrong. There isn't anything we can't get through together. I promise."

From the day her mom died, she wanted to take the sadness out of her father's eyes. To be the one who put even more there, it tore her heart apart.

"I'm so sorry, Daddy." He pulled up into one of the chairs. Like a little girl of seven, she sat in his lap, protected in his arms.

Her stomach quivered. One deep breath and it all came out. She told him about Tommy and the baby. About her fears. She told him about the old boyfriend who took everything from her. She even told him about her conflicted feelings about Adrian. Years of not talking to her father came to an end.

His arms tightened, holding her closer. Not one word passed his lips. Exhausted, she rested her cheek against his shoulder. Her tears fell on her arm. Sitting up, to wipe them away, she realized they belonged to her father.

She cupped his face, just as he had done to her, and an image flashed in her brain. Her father's tears, and her tiny hands holding his face. "Don't cry, Daddy. I'll be good. I promise." She had broken her promise.

The warmth of his long fingers brought her back to the present. "I'm so sorry, Daddy. I messed up and made it worse by hiding it from everyone."

"We all make mistakes." He gave her his secret grin she loved. "I married Sheila, but we have Samantha because of her. There's a family that was formed because of your decisions."

Love for this man who raised her and loved her exploded her heart into pieces. The words not said over the years were understood. She wrapped her arms around him and hugged him as if she was still the little girl who wanted to make everything right in a torn world. "I love you, Daddy. I'm so sorry."

She was curled up in his lap, and his long arms pulled her closer. "Shh. None of that nonsense. I'm so happy you're home. I love you so much, baby girl." Large hands cradled her head. He pressed his cheek against hers. "I'm the one who's sorry."

In the middle of the old room, surrounded by decades of forgotten chairs, they sat in silence. For over a decade, she had been lost without even knowing it. Maybe God brought her home for this very reason. Closing her eyes, she took in the comforting smell of home and love. *Thank You, God.*

For the first time in twelve years, her heart settled. Her world was stabilizing. Except for the feelings she had for Adrian. What could she do about those? She doubted he would celebrate her decision to give up her son after what she'd witnessed with Charlotte arriving back in his life.

He wouldn't understand why she chose to give her baby to another family. With a sigh, she settled against her father's heartbeat. She'd worry about that later. Right now, she just wanted to be the little girl wrapped up in her daddy's arms.

Chapter Nine

Adrian glanced at his daughter. The yellow ribbon that tied off her braid had slipped loose and threatened to fall off. He reached over and quickly retied it. Looking up at him, she smiled. Yeah, he tended to worry and be overprotective, but wasn't that a dad's job? He rested his hand on her small shoulder and squeezed.

When he'd told her that her mother had visited and had given him a letter for her, he'd expected her to want to read it. Instead she narrowed her eyes and stared at him for a long while before asking what he wanted her to do.

That had caught him off guard. What did he want? He wanted Charlotte to go back wherever she came from and stay out of their lives. He had hesitated. Closing his eyes, he had prayed for the right words. None came, so he told her he wasn't sure how he felt.

"Earth to Dad." Mia lightly jabbed him with her elbow.

He glanced around. People were getting up from the pews. George laughed. "I think he might be distracted." He nodded to the pew in the front, where the Bergmann sisters sat.

"Dad, I said you need to stop by Fred's Tacos and get some of the barbacoa for your date. Lizzy says it's her aunt's favorite thing to eat."

"It's not a—"

"Hey, *mija*. Are you ready to do some shopping?" His sister Leti hugged Mia from the back. With her arms around her, she rested her chin on his daughter's head. "You're getting taller!"

"Shopping? I thought you were going to the children's museum." He scowled at his sister. He budgeted their shopping trips and he didn't have the extra money right now unless he went into his savings.

"Oh, stop scowling at me. If a single, hard-working woman can't splurge on her favorite niece, what good is it?" She looked down at Mia. "Are you ready?"

A sweet giggle came from his daughter. He hoped she never outgrew that sound. "I'm your only niece."

She shrugged. "I'm sure you would be my favorite if I had twenty. Let's go."

"Yes, ma'am. As soon as I know Daddy is set. He's going on a date with Nikki."

"It's not a date." He tried to keep his voice low so others wouldn't overhear. "We're just going riding over her mother's ranch." All three sets of brown eyes looked at him as if they didn't believe a word of it. He sighed and scanned the room for Nikki. He really wanted to get on his horse and get away from all the people who wanted to meddle in his life. Somehow, she had become the calm spot in the midst of his storms.

"I just don't want you to mess this up, Daddy."

George laughed. "Oh, he will."

Sometimes he really didn't like his brother. Leti took Mia's hand. "Remember to have fun, Adrian, and smile. Women like it when you smile." She winked at George.

Before Leti got too far, Adrian reached for her arm and leaned in close, so no one would hear. "Let her talk about her mother if she wants, and be nice. Don't say anything negative. Just let Mia talk."

His sister's face tightened with a stiff nod. She put her arms around Mia, and they walked off. An empty feeling gripped him as he watched them leave. They were going to Kerrville. What if they ran into Charlotte?

"Hi, George. Adrian."

He turned and found Nikki standing there.

She wore a soft green dress that swirled when she walked. He tried to remember if he'd ever seen her in a dress before today. Her hair was down, falling around her neck and brushing her shoulders.

"Hey, Nikki." George gave her a quick hug. "You kids have a wonderful day. I'm heading to Uvalde. See you tonight. Maybe we can all have dinner together." With a wink, he punched Adrian then left them standing there, alone.

She crossed her arms over her waist then dropped them only to put them back. "I went to get coffee, and my family left me. I guess they thought I was going directly to the ranch with you."

He chuckled. "My family made sure I was alone too. Family. Can't live with them, and you can't, well…shoot them. I'm parked out back." He held out his hand to help her down the steps.

Her first reaction was to pull away. Then he heard her take a deep breath. She smiled and put her hand in his. "Thank you."

Progress. He started whistling.

Falling into step next to him, Nikki tried to figure the best way to ask about Mia and Charlotte. It had been on her brain all night and day. It was probably the closest she had ever been to continuous prayer.

He opened his truck door for her and once again offered up a hand. This time she smiled for real. It didn't even occur to him she might be offended.

Of course, today she did feel a little different. Her sisters dressed her up for church and she wasn't sure how she felt about it. As soon as she could, she would change her clothes. *Oh no, my bag. They took off with—*

"I'm thinking this belongs to you." He lifted her backpack from the bed of his truck.

"How thoughtful of them to drop off my things after abandoning me." Her sisters were working overtime getting her together with Adrian.

As he slipped into the driver's seat, he passed the bag over to her. Then his focus turned to driving. In his starched blue button-up shirt and jeans, he looked so handsome.

"Mia didn't read the letter."

His voice pulled her out of her daydreams. "What?"

He glanced at her. "I told Mia about Charlotte and our visit yesterday."

"What did she say?"

"She asked me what I thought and how I felt. When I told her I wasn't sure, she nodded and said she didn't know either. She asked if she could hold the letter for now. She said she'd let me know when she was ready to read it."

"Are you happy about her reaction?"

A half-hearted chuckle lifted his solid shoulders. "It's a relief to have talked with her. I was so afraid of her being hurt, I avoided the topic. Looking back, I'm sure it had a lot to do with my own anger. When I'm working with the teen parents, I talk to them about dealing with emotions honestly. I encourage them to take the time to dig down into the root of the emotion. Is it jealousy, anger or pride? It's so much easier to point out others' splinters."

As they went through town, people waved. Adrian would give the two-finger wave from the top of his steering wheel.

She sighed. "That's what Pastor John talked about today."

"Yep. Amazing all the ways God will talk to you if you're listening."

Watching the town disappear into open pastures and hills, Nikki adjusted her seat belt. "I'm not sure He talks to me anymore. This is the first time I've been to church since I left Clear Water."

"Really? You know He's not just hanging out in church. He's everywhere, and He's always talking. We just let all the other voices and business of life keep us distracted. On the ranch, in the saddle, is where I hear Him the most."

She was pretty sure He would've been yelling at her anyway. *Go home, Nikki. Tell the truth, Nikki. Apologize to everyone you hurt, Nikki.* She closed her eyes.She needed her own twelve-step program. Maybe that was just her guilt talking and not God.

God, I'm home and I have told the truth to my family. What now? They passed her mother's family ranch. The gate was still locked. It was hard to think of it as her ranch. Her father hated the place.

The massive Childress entry gate loomed on the horizon. Adrian turned into the ranch road, his hands sure and steady on the steering wheel. She even loved the way his hands moved.

Before contemplating a real relationship with him, she needed to decide where she was going. It wasn't just about them. It would also affect his daughter.

After spending time watching the growing fawn play and take her bottle, Adrian had walked Nikki to the barn and saddled the horses.

Now they were deep into the Cortez original homestead. At one time, it was one of the largest ranches. After generations of families divided and split it up, however, Nikki and her sisters only had about seven hundred acres. Even at that, Adrian couldn't imagine owning a property like this, let alone having it handed to you. It was such a waste, allowing it to go untended.

Adrian settled into the saddle. He checked Zeta again. She tossed her head, not liking the slow pace Tank was traveling.

"Adrian De La Cruz, you put me on a baby-sitter horse, didn't you?" She nudged the red-spotted Appaloosa and flicked the reins, trying with no success to get the gelding to move faster than a slow walk. He twisted his ears back and forth, but kept his head down and his hooves plodding. "I can't believe you didn't trust me enough to put me on a real horse."

He pulled Zeta up and looked at Nikki. "And as you say that, you're trying to move him out. He's a good and safe horse for someone recovering from knee surgery."

"I've never moved so slow in my life."

"Maybe it's time for you to slow down and take in the scenery around you. I think your mom's family ranch is one of the most beautiful pieces of property in the canyon. It's a shame that your dad has locked it down. The juniper will take over soon if it's not cleared. Some of the outbuildings might already be lost."

"I know. Danica and Jackie said he won't talk about it." She urged Tank to move faster again, but he swished his tail in response. "Open communication does not run rapid in the Bergmann household."

"Have you thought about talking to him? I know you want to go back to the Grand Canyon, but have you thought about doing something similar here? Between the cliffs and river, you could run all sorts of adventure packages from here. Hiking, biking, horseback riding, along with kayaking. Throw some cabins out here and you'll have people from San Antonio and Houston on a waiting list."

She shook her head and grinned at him. "Now you sound like the twins. Did they put you up to this?"

"They might have mentioned it in passing, but they didn't tell me to tell you. I like the idea of you staying around Clear Water." He realized he wanted to spend more time with her. "I'd miss you." The breeze felt cool against the flash of heat that burned his face.

Standing in the stirrups, he twisted a bit to watch Nikki. He loved the slight scowl she had as she tried to talk Tank into moving faster.

For the first time, he was interested in what the future would be like with a woman in his life. With Nikki. Mia liked her, and the idea of a relationship didn't scare him.

He lowered his head as the narrow path took

them under a bent live oak that created a canopy. Past the live-oak grove, it opened to a field full of native pecan trees. The grass was lush and green with the river a few yards away. He could hear the running water, and the cypresses were visible, but he couldn't see the river.

"We're close to my favorite spot." She pulled Tank to a stop and stood in the saddle. Turning her head, she surveyed the area. "It's been so long. I think it's right up there. I hope it looks the same. Floods have a way of changing the landscape." Clicking her tongue, she put Tank back into motion. Slow motion, but he was moving forward. With a heavy sigh, Zeta followed.

He patted her withers. "Good girl. I promise later today we can run and play with the cattle."

"I take it Tank does not play with the cattle?" She leaned over his neck. "What if I promise you some molasses on your feed?" The spotted ears flicked back as if he was willing to consider it.

Adrian laughed. "The last thing that horse needs is molasses."

As the path lowered, the river came into view. Nikki stood up in her stirrups again. "There it is. That's where we would swim and hang out on warm days." She turned back to him, her face alive with excitement. "It was Mom's favorite place during the summer. With her chair in the edge of the water, she'd read while we played and swam."

Two gentle slopes flattened on the water's edge, creating a little sandy beach surrounded by the rocks. It was different than any other area he'd ever seen on the river, and he'd covered many miles in a tube or kayak. "This is a great spot. It's amazing no one knows about it."

"My mom's family was small and very private. My grandfather didn't allow friends out here. He said they'd start thinking they could come whenever they wanted and bring more people." She gave a half chuckle. "He didn't like people. Loved animals, but could do without people. Except for us. He loved us." She became still and stared out across the overgrown pastures. "I miss him."

Adrian didn't know what to say. He hadn't lost anyone close in his family. "I remember his funeral. My dad worked for him a few seasons. He had a lot of respect for your grandfather. I was a freshman, so you were a senior when he died?"

She nodded and dismounted, making her way to the largest pecan tree. Dead branches were tangled throughout the tree, strangling the healthy ones. Nikki always seemed to have it all together. She lost her grandfather at the same time the trouble her father was having with his

second wife led to an ugly divorce from her
stepmother. All he remembered was the bold
smile she always had on her face, and the fierce
determination in every movement when he
watched her play sports.

He figured the smile hid a great deal of loss
and pain. He dismounted and followed her. Letters were carved into the tree trunk. Her fingers traced the grooves. "He carved each of our
names in the tree when we turned five. He said
it was so the land would not forget us and we
would not forget we belonged here." She pressed
her palm flat against the tree's rough bark. Silence settled between them. Then her shoulders
trembled.

She was crying. The deep silent internal kind
of grief that consumed a body. Not knowing
what else to do, he moved close enough to wrap
her in his arms. If nothing else, she needed to
know she wasn't alone.

The breeze gently stirred loose strands of
long hair against his skin. Turning, she buried
her face between his shoulder and neck. Not
a sound was made, but his shirt was wet. His
heart broke. Birds flew from tree to tree, the
horses munched on the green grass and the river
flowed around rocks and over roots as he held
her.

If there was a way to take the pain he would,

but he knew it was her grief and she would have to deal with it. He suspected that was the problem. For years she had been running, climbing and jumping, not facing the loss.

After a while, she stepped back and wiped her face with the backs of her hands. "I'm so sorry. I don't know what happened. I never cry." Looking off in the distance, she crossed her arms over her waist. "I don't know what's wrong with me."

"It's okay to cry." He knew it was bad when she started chewing on her lip. He'd never seen her do that. "You've lost people you love. There's nothing wrong with grieving." He wanted to tell her the only thing about her that wasn't perfect was her plan to leave, but it wasn't the time for that kind of confession. "Maybe some barbacoa from Fred's Tacos would help you feel better. I happen to have a couple of tacos with your name on them."

Her face relaxed into a smile. "Really? I love those. They're my favorite."

"That's what I hear." Getting the foil-wrapped tacos out of the saddlebag, he handed her a couple. "You want to go sit on the rock over there?" He pointed to the edge of the river. Between two cypresses that towered over the river, there was a large flat rock tangled in the roots. Water lapped against it.

He reached out and offered his hand to her. For a stuttering heartbeat, he thought she wasn't going to take it. With a shy smile, her fingers wrapped around his and he helped her over the uneven terrain of rocks and roots along the way to the flat limestone.

"When I was a kid, I would sit on this rock for hours if my mom let me." Nikki took a deep breath and closed her eyes.

Watching her had become one of his favorite pastimes. "I can't imagine you ever sitting for hours."

Hands on her hips, she turned to stare into the clear water of the Frio. "That is probably true. It might have been minutes, but it was the only time I remember sitting still and being content."

Adrian unrolled the small blanket tucked under his arm and sat down, leaning against the old cypress. He rested his arm across his raised knee. "I think I might actually be able to sit and relax here too. You're blessed to have this place. I can't believe you stayed away so long. You couldn't have dragged me past the fence line." Unwrapping his soft taco, he nodded to her.

Sighing as if the world sat on her shoulders, Nikki joined him on the colorful Mexican blanket and started eating the barbacoa he'd bought for her.

For a while they ate in silence, just the sounds of God's creation surrounding them. She paused in the middle of her second taco and looked at him. "I was angry and guilty. At the time I thought it was better if I left. Then it just got harder to come back." She gave him the gift of her smile. "You're the kind that stands firm and waits it out. You've done a great job with your daughter. You're a rare man, Adrian De La Cruz." Her gaze turned to the pecan grove where the horses grazed. "Most men would have run earlier when I had my little meltdown, or at least told me it was going to be all right with a pat on the back." She lifted her shoulders, and her summer blues stared straight at him. "Thank you for just holding me."

He leaned forward and took her hand. "Grief and other emotions stay with us, even when we try to bury them. That's a lesson you just witnessed me learning yesterday. I was returning the favor. You stayed when I was at my worst."

Nikki moved closer. "It just made you more human. I was worried for a while that you were too perfect." Her eyes danced with light.

One hard laugh came up from his gut. "No, that would be you." An electric wire ran through his veins, connected to her. He cupped her face, and the wire went live. "I've known you were perfect since I was thirteen years old and thought you were the love of my life."

Confusion creased her brow.

That invisible wire reeled him in until he was less than an inch from her. All those years ago he knew what he wanted, but he hadn't acted. "I thought you were out of my reach. Then you left without warning, Nicole Bergmann, and broke my heart."

He loved her in high school?

Finally, he moved in to kiss her.

This time he was gonna follow through on the promise his eyes made several times. From the determination stamped in his jaw, nothing was going to stop him this time.

The light stubble along the edge of his jawbone tickled her fingers as she encouraged him to come closer. His dark eyes with the depth of the universe dropped to meet hers. Her breath froze in her lungs. Then he kissed her and fire melted her very core.

Adrian De La Cruz was kissing her. Kissing her on her secret river rock.

She tasted peppermint and spices. Firm and powerful, his mouth took what he wanted. Joy bubbled at the thought of this beautiful man waiting for her for so long. She could stay here in his arms forever.

He broke from the kiss and rested his forehead on hers, breathing as if he'd just roped a calf in record time. Could a heart tremble? Hers was doing something strange, something she had never experienced before this moment. Warning bells went off in her head.

"I want you to stay in Clear Water." His words were a pickax to the already weak heart.

Closing her eyes, she took the scent and warmth of him into her small protected world. "Adrian—"

The song "Kiss the Girl" started playing from his pocket. She sat back and raised one brow. Adrian's tanned skin actually went darker as he grabbed for his phone. "That's it! She's never getting a phone or leaving her room." He put the phone to his ear, slightly turning away from Nikki.

"Mia, you need to leave my phone alone. It's not funny."

She couldn't help but laugh. "It is kind of funny," she whispered.

Adrian shot her a hard glare.

"I'll ask her. Seriously, Mia, don't mess with my phone or you'll never get your own." Slipping the phone back in his pocket, he looked at her from under his thick lashes.

"Sorry. She must have changed it this morning." He stood and offered his hand to help her up. "George has invited you to dinner. There's a game on tonight and, well, they want you to join us."

Face-to-face, he tucked his knuckle under her chin. "I would love for you to have dinner at our house tonight." He leaned in for another kiss. The first one was fire and ice.

This one was a light breeze across her lips. "Will you let me feed you dinner?"

She nodded. Where had the gravity gone? His warmth disappeared. Her anchor left her. She opened her eyes and found him walking toward the pecan trees.

He turned back to her, leading the horses. "I'll take that as a yes?"

She smiled and nodded again, getting up to join him.

"I need to get some work in on the Childress's horses. It won't take long. Then we can head to my house. Do you mind?" He helped her mount without even asking if she needed help.

What surprised her was that she was starting to like it. Anyone else and she would have put a stop to that nonsense, but being close to Adrian felt right.

With one hand on her braced knee, he looked up at her. "Is the knee okay?"

She nodded again.

He laughed. "My mother used to offer me

money to not talk. I never made it to the end of the timer. You would have raked in the dough. Let me get the blanket. Then it's to the boss's stables. Ready?"

"I'm ready." Was she? Was she ready to risk it all for another man?

Chapter Ten

Nikki eased the door open. It was late and she didn't want to bother anyone who had turned in for the night.

"Nikki, is that you?" Her dad's voice emanated from the kitchen. Then she heard giggling. Giggling? It didn't sound like one of her sisters.

"Dad?" Carrying her boots in one hand and her backpack over her shoulder, she stepped into the large family kitchen. Lorrie Ann's mother, Sonia Ortega, sat at the table with him. They each had a plate full of pecan pie and vanilla ice cream.

Sonia stood up. "Sit, sit, sit. I'll fix you a plate. The pie is still warm." She paused in slicing and looked at Nikki. "One or two scoops."

"Uh, one." She slid into the chair next to her dad. Why was Sonia Ortega hanging out with her dad at ten o'clock at night? "What are you doing here?"

"Nicole." Her father gave her the look.

"Sorry, I didn't mean to be rude. I've just—"

Ms. Ortega waved her hand. "Oh, don't worry about it, *mija*. I saw your father at the store picking up one of those frozen pies—" she shuddered "—and I couldn't let a good man eat one of those dreadful things. I offered to bring him a homemade one. He said only if he could cook me dinner." She set the pecan pie and semi-melted ice cream in front of her. "He made steaks, and I brought the pie."

"All the girls just went upstairs. The twins have school in the morning."

Nikki tried to keep her face neutral. The stupid eyebrow wanted to pop up, but that might look rude. When did her father start keeping company with Sonia Ortega?

To stop things from getting awkward, she shoved a fork full of... Oh, my. She might have moaned. Sonia smiled at her and her father chuckled. "Good, isn't it?"

She nodded and took another bite to make sure it tasted the way she thought it tasted the first time. Another moan escaped. "This is the best pecan pie I've ever tasted. You made this?" Oh, that sounded rude. "I mean, I know your sister owns the Pecan Farm and makes a mean pie, and the other one has the bakery, but this is a whole other experience."

With red cheeks, Sonia nodded. "To be fair, Maggie and Maria did teach me how to bake. It's become a hobby. They've asked me to join in the business."

"I was thinking they could run it out of the upstairs area once the De La Cruz boys finish it." Her father popped another forkful in his mouth.

This time she couldn't stop both eyebrows from showing her surprise. "Uh…have you talked to the twins about this?"

He scowled at her. "It's my building and my business."

"We haven't even talked about it. I wouldn't do anything to cause problems." Sonia tucked her long hair behind her ear and took another bite, keeping her eyes down.

She thought of how Sheila had taken advantage of her father right after the death of her mother. She didn't know much about Sonia other than she had left her daughter to be raised by Maggie Shultz, Sonia's sister. The Ortega family was one of the most solid families, but Sonia had had problems with alcohol and drugs in the past. Sounded too much like Sheila for her comfort.

"You're home later than expected." Her father's gruff voice brought back the reason she tried to sneak into the house. "You and Adrian dating now?"

"Daddy, just because we went riding on the ranch and had dinner with his brother and daughter doesn't mean we're dating. We're just friends, like you and Sonia."

He narrowed his gaze. "Friends are good. Have you decided to stay, or will you be going back to the Grand Canyon?"

"I haven't decided. Thank you for the pie. I'm going to bed. It's been a long day, and my knee is feeling it." Did she just use her knee as an excuse?

Her knee did feel a bit sore and stiff as she slowly took the steps one at a time. Slipping into her old bedroom, she found Danica and Jackie waiting for her.

"So?"

"You stayed all day!"

"Did he kiss you?"

"Do you have another date?"

"They do! Thursday, right? What are you going to wear?"

Nikki held her hands up in surrender and laughed. "One question at a time, please?" She dropped her backpack and boots then fell flat on her bed. If she was going to stay, she'd have to get a new comforter. The purple-and-black polka dots had to go.

The twins flopped on their bellies with her in the middle. "So did he kiss you?"

She giggled. They squealed. Then covered their mouths, expressions identical. Danica glanced at the door. "Shh. I don't want the girls to wake up."

Jackie hunched her shoulders and rested her chin in her palms. "You have to tell us everything."

"I don't have to tell you anything. He's very private, and I don't think I should talk about him. But I do want to talk about Dad. What's up with Sonia being over here for dinner? Do y'all know her well? Are they dating?"

"I'd much rather talk about you and Adrian." Danica sat up, crossed her legs and leaned against the white headboard. "Dad hasn't dated since Sheila left, and this is the first time Sonia has come over for dinner. No one's been at the house since I brought Reid home, so it's kinda nice." She shrugged. "I don't really know her well, other than she's an Ortega and had a drinking or drug problem, but she's been sober for years now. She's been in town more now that Lorrie Ann is expecting. You know she's Lorrie Ann's real mom?"

"Yeah. Wait! Lorrie Ann's pregnant? How far? She doesn't look like it."

"Six months, which is totally unfair. I was waddling by four months." Danica crossed her arms.

"You were carrying twins." Jackie looked at Nikki. "When did you start showing?"

The question threw her for a moment. She never thought about that time in her life. It was easier to pretend it didn't exist. She ran her hand over her taut midsection. "At six months I could still hide it. I think it wasn't until eight that I couldn't wear jeans anymore, and all my shirts were tight."

"Was it hard? Do you think about him a lot?"

She stared at the ceiling. Posters of all her high school celebrity crushes hung there staring back at her.

"I haven't told Adrian." Her throat suddenly hurt. The words didn't flow easily.

"Do you think he'll be angry you didn't tell him?"

"After watching his reaction to Charlotte, I'm not sure how he'll feel." Well, she was, and that was what scared her. She really needed to get over this fear of disappointing people and just learn to deal with the consequences.

"You have to tell him. If he isn't supportive and can't understand what you did was an unselfish act of love, then he doesn't deserve you." Danica leaned forward and tucked a strand of Nikki's stray curls behind her ear.

It was an act their mom had done a million times when they were little. The urge to cry gripped her heart. No, she was done with tears. "I think I've hesitated because I'm afraid of his disappointment, and I'm still not sure how I feel about it. I don't think of it as the unselfish act you think it was."

Both sisters wrapped her in their arms. Danica sat back and looked Nikki in the eye. "Have you gotten any counseling?"

All she could do was shake her head.

Jackie whispered close to her ear. "You need to talk to a professional."

Danica took her hand. "There's the Hill Country Pregnancy Care Center. We've volunteered there, and our church has financially supported them. They have counselors who can help you sort through your feelings. I know as Bergmanns we're taught at an early age to avoid emotions because they're messy and ugly. It would've been better if Mom had been around, but she wasn't. If you're going to have any kind of real future, you need to be okay with this."

Jackie played with Nikki's hair. "A future I hope includes us. Please don't leave us again. We just got you back, and we want to keep you."

Nikki nodded and swallowed the hard knot in her throat. Would Adrian want to have a future with her if he knew about her past?

Chapter Eleven

Adrian lowered his gaze a bit and made sure eighteen-year-old Nathan looked him in the eye. He held the handshake firm and waited. The new father sighed and nodded. "Yes, sir. I'll call if I need anything."

With a nod, Adrian let go of the young man's hand. "You're not alone. It will get overwhelming, but you've made a commitment for the long haul. They're counting on you to be a man now. If you start wanting to run or walk out, call me. I'll help you through it. I've been there. I know how scary it can be when they need you and you don't know if you can do it."

"Thank you, Mr. De La Cruz." Seventeen-year-old Jazmine stood at the door with their newborn daughter on her hip. The young father joined her and took the baby. One smile and they were gone.

Adrian closed his eyes and covered them in prayer. With a sigh, he started packing the refreshments Karly had brought. Just a few carrots and water bottles were left. Her husband, Tyler Childress, had called during their meeting because her son had fallen and cut open his forehead, again.

He told her to go and he'd take care of everything. After putting away the chairs, he hit the switch with his free hand. Turning down the hallway, he almost dropped the box.

"Nikki?" She was the last person he expected to see at the pregnancy center. "What are you doing here?"

She had the look of a wild animal caught in a trap. Her eyes wide, she stared at him before darting her gaze around the hall. Was she looking for an escape?

"Are you okay? Do you need help?"

Her breathing slowed and she gave him a tight smile. "I think I'm lost. I was looking for the door to the north parking lot."

"You're in the wrong hall. If you want to walk with me, I gotta put these in the kitchen then I'm heading that way. Are you with Jackie?" The twins had helped with event planning in the past, but he couldn't figure out why Nikki was here and acting strange. "Nikki, I enjoyed Sunday. I'd love to do it again." He gave a bit of time to reply, which she didn't, so he plowed ahead. "I thought I'd pick you up at six for our Thursday-night music night."

Big blue eyes just stared at him, as if he spoke gibberish. Or she was thinking of a polite way to turn him down.

When he'd taken her home, he would've told anyone who asked that she enjoyed herself as much as he had. Maybe the kiss freaked her out. She made it clear she didn't want to get emotionally involved, but now he was getting mixed signals. "Have you decided to volunteer here?"

"No." Hands in her pockets, she rocked on the balls of her feet as he shifted the case of water to the other arm. "I came to talk to a counselor Danica recommended."

Standing there, he turned to her. Now he was concerned. "Are you…?"

Her eyes went wide and she shook her head. "No! I have something that I needed to talk to someone about that…" She looked away from him. Her breathing went up a notch. "Before we talk about another date, I need to tell you something." Her long legs ate up the length of the hallway as she moved ahead of him. "For anyone else it might not make a difference, but with your own history, I think it might be a game changer."

Stopping in the lobby area, she looked around.

She probably just realized she didn't know where she was going when she took the lead. He stepped past her and opened the door to the kitchen area.

"Hey, Adrian." One of the program staff sat at the table. She smiled and made small chit-chat. Then, gathering some supplies, she said 'bye and left.

He started stacking water bottles in the refrigerator. "What did you want to talk about?" He glanced over his shoulder.

Nikki had the don't-get-close-to-me look in place. She scanned the hallway. "Maybe in the parking lot?"

"Sure." He chuckled, trying to lighten the mood. "Sounds like top secret stuff. I used to pretend I was a spy. I made George be the Russian spy."

A half smile pulled at one side of her mouth. "Nothing so dramatic."

They walked in silence as they made their way through the corridors. Adrian tried to imagine what she needed to say that would involve the pregnancy center.

Hands in her pockets, she had yet to look at him. "You're a counselor to the pregnant teens?"

"No, I'm one of the mentors to the teens that are parents. The counselors work with them when they first come in. If they decide to keep the baby, they suggest they become part of the support group. I mainly work with the teen dads and sometimes the grandparents."

"Do you ever work with the parents who give the babies up for adoption?"

"No. I know it's one of the options the counselors talk about, but I just mentor the ones that want to raise their baby." Her father's truck was across the now-empty parking lot. Adrian stopped in front of her door. "So what does this have to do with what you want to talk to me about?"

She crossed her arms and looked to the empty playground. "Before you ask me out again, I think it would be fair for you to know the truth."

Leaning against the truck, he waited. A slight tug at his gut made him uncomfortable. He really liked Nikki and didn't want anything to change that.

Shifting from one leg to another, she flexed the knee with the brace.

"Is your knee hurting? We can go sit on the picnic tables."

"No, no. It's fine." A breeze rustled the leaves in the giant live-oak trees. A sliver of the sun's last rays hung over the hilltops, casting pinks and red across the clouds. Nikki seemed fascinated with the colors in the sky.

"Nikki. Whatever it is, just tell me. You saw

me at my worst on Saturday, and you didn't run screaming for the hills. I can handle it, and we can go from there."

He reached out and tucked away a loose strand of hair that was caught in her eyelashes.

She looked at the ground and nodded. "The reason I left Clear Water was because I was pregnant, and I didn't want my father or sisters to know. I was too ashamed."

He straightened. It couldn't be true. "That was the beginning of your senior year." He tried to think back to whom she was dating. "I don't remember you being with anyone."

She turned away from him and shrugged. "That doesn't matter. He didn't want anything to do with the baby. I was so ashamed. I went to my great-aunt Gloria, my mother's aunt. She helped me take care of everything." Lips firm, she locked her gaze with his. "I gave my baby up for adoption. It was the best option for us at the time."

Everything inside him froze. He couldn't have heard right. "You gave your baby away?"

"Aunt Gloria had a grandson that was married, and they weren't able to have a child. She went to them first. They were so grateful to have the baby. It was an open adoption, but only recently could I handle thinking about him."

His heart was pounding in his ears. A headache was starting. Rubbing his face didn't make it go away. "So like Charlotte, you walked out and just went back to life like nothing happened?" He couldn't believe this.

After all the years, the first woman he was interested in exploring a future with, and she turned out just like Charlotte. What was wrong with him?

He didn't want to say anything he'd regret. Taking a deep breath and relaxing his jaw, Adrian pulled his truck keys out of his pocket. "Thanks for telling me. I have to go get Mia from my mom's."

"Adrian?"

He turned back to her, his jaw tight again. He looked over her shoulder to the sun disappearing. He had no business feeling betrayed, but he did. "When are you heading back to Arizona?" He could use some distance from her right now.

A long silence fell between them. Then she answered. "I told Mia I'd be here for the July rodeo to watch her ride."

"She's only gonna hurt more when you leave. I'd appreciate it if you didn't encourage a friendship with her. She has enough to deal with right now because of Charlotte showing back up in our lives."

"I wouldn't do anything to hurt her. I—"

"You might not mean to, but I think it's best

if you keep your distance from now on. I'll
see you around." He couldn't stand there any
longer without wanting to yell. How did some
people find it so easy to walk away? Was it
just the way they were wired? Was it because
of her mother's death? Or her father's marriage
to Sheila?

All he knew was he couldn't afford to have
someone he loved walk out on him again. And
this time Mia was old enough to feel the pain.

He glanced in his rearview mirror to make
sure she got in the truck and it started. What
he saw took his breath. Nikki leaned over the
steering wheel, her shoulders shaking. It looked
as if she was sobbing.

Changing gears, he was about to turn around
and go back to her. But she lifted her head and
he realized she was talking on the phone. He
waited. Should he go offer her help? Would it
be better if she didn't know he saw her crying? One thing he knew about her: she hated
to look weak.

After one last glance to reassure himself she
would be all right, he put the truck in Drive and
headed home. Relationships complicated life.

Mia wanted him to date so he'd have someone in his life when she grew up. That thought
didn't sit well with him. One day, she'd want

to bring some boy to the house, and the idea of her dating just about made his heart break all over again.

Nikki wiped her face and focused on her sister's voice. She hated crying. "Kristine was great. Thank you for setting up the appointment. But by chance did you happen to know Adrian would be here tonight?"

There was a slight pause over the connection. "I might have. Did you see him? Did he ask you out?"

Nikki tilted her head back. "I was feeling pretty good after talking with the counselor, so I thought I might as well tell Adrian too. I don't want any more secrets hovering over my life."

"How did it go?" Danica's voice was low and soft.

"About the way I expected. He compared me to Charlotte and asked that I stay away from Mia. He says he doesn't want her hurt when I leave."

"That was a jerk move on his part, but I know Adrian. Once he settles down and thinks about it, he'll understand and feel bad. Are you still leaving? Did you tell him you were thinking about staying?"

"It's not about me going back to Arizona—he

sees me as a woman who abandoned her child. Just like Charlotte abandoned him and Mia."

"It's not the same."

"It kind of is. She left Mia with someone who she knew would love her daughter and take care of her. That's the exact same thing I did. It was the right choice for all of us. My only regret was not telling you and Daddy. I should have come home sooner."

"You're home now. If Adrian doesn't understand and wants to be a jerk about it, then that's his problem and he's missing out on one incredible woman. His loss. Why are men so stupid?"

"Why do we keep loving them?"

"So maybe we're the stupid ones." Danica sighed. "I know God has a plan. It's all for the good. It has to be."

"I would really like being in on the plan. I'm heading home. Do you need me to stop and get anything?"

"Nope. Just you. I love that you're home. I really hope you think about making it work here. Even without Adrian, I think this is a good place for you to be."

"I've been praying about it. Like you said, with or without Adrian, I'm liking the possibilities and opportunities I have in Clear Water." She turned the key and the diesel engine rumbled to life. "We'll talk when I get home."

After a quick goodbye, Nikki put the truck in Drive and turned toward home.

Adrian kept popping up in her head no matter how hard she tried to think of something else, anything else.

Would she be able to stay here and build a business and a new life with Adrian so close? She wouldn't be able to avoid him in a town this small. *God, I'm open to Your will. I've been lost, and now I turn my life over to You. Show me the path You want me to take.*

Silence filled her head. A calm silence. With a deep sigh, she relaxed. She was where she needed to be right now. If Adrian had a problem with the choices she'd made as a young girl, then that was on him. Her sister was right. She deserved someone who loved her completely, flaws and all. The way she loved him.

Love. Had she fallen in love with Adrian De La Cruz? This was not good.

Chapter Twelve

George whistled as he surveyed the physical results of Adrian's anger. "Brother, you did a number on the room. Man, I had no idea you had all this suppressed." He studied his twin. "It's kind of scary."

Uncomfortable, Adrian leaned against the door frame and looked at the table Nikki had restored. He didn't like the person he had become over the last week, and George would see right through any lie.

"Are you sure you're okay? This is worse than I imagined. Really, Adrian. If I hadn't seen this, I would think all was good with you." He walked over and picked up a broken piece of the old wall. "Nikki saw this firsthand, and she still went on a date with you? That girl is tough."

"She read the letter and suggested that I talk

to Mia right away. My first instinct was to burn the letter and never tell my daughter."

George rolled his eyes. "That would have worked out well. And that was sarcasm, in case you misunderstood." He dropped the drywall and dusted off his hands. "I'm sure she would've been pretty mad when she found out Charlotte had been in town." He walked through the rubble. "You haven't mentioned Nikki other than you had a great time together. Are you going out again? Sunday night was fun with all of us hanging out. That would make your daughter happy." He glanced at the door. "I wonder where Nikki is. She's usually here before us."

Adrian ran his hand through his hair. "She might be avoiding me."

George looked up from the pile he started under the window. "What did you do?"

"Why is it my fault? There are certain things I can't live with."

His twin stopped what he was doing and narrowed his gaze at Adrian. "You know you can be a self-righteous jerk at times, right? I mean, I love you and all, but none of us are perfect. Not even you, little brother."

The wood of the table was warm as Adrian ran his fingers along the grain. Was he being a jerk? Probably. "I'm just feeling...I don't know. Raw?" He rubbed his forehead. "With Charlotte showing up without warning, I feel like I'm caught up in a tornado."

"Don't be an idiot. Nikki isn't Charlotte."

"She's made it clear she wants to leave. I don't want my daughter hurt again by another woman walking out on her."

"Mia is fine. You're the one with the problem. Stop hiding behind your daughter and take a chance. What could she have done that's worth giving up on her?"

"I don't want to talk about it." It wasn't his place to tell Nikki's private business. "Let's just say we had a disagreement and I—"

Boots hit the top of the steps and both men turned to look. Nikki strode across the room. She didn't make eye contact. "Hi, George. Adrian."

"Hey, Nikki." Nose in the air, George took a big whiff. "I think I smell my favorite food group." He raised an eyebrow to his twin and tilted his head.

The aroma of fresh-roasted coffee filled the room as Nikki set the large cups on the table. "I thought with the major cleanup in front of you today, I'd bring coffee from the Daily Grind."

"You're a true gift. You're gonna make some jerk a happy man one day." George dropped the broken pieces of drywall and walked past his brother to get to the tall cup of hot caffeine. He elbowed Adrian as he passed him and gave him the "you are an idiot" look. He picked up a cup and took a deep sip.

After a satisfied sigh, he turned to Nikki. "I hear from Danica you might be opening your adventure-guide business here in Clear Water. You know the competition at the Grand Canyon would be tough, but we need something like that here. All we have is tube rentals. You'd make a killing. Right, Adrian?"

Adrian narrowed his eyes at the brother he would rather smack than agree with, but he'd let his temper get the better part of him lately. "Yeah, I could see it working, but you have to do what makes you happy. Don't let siblings alter what you see as your future." He swallowed and turned his back to them. He didn't realize how much it would hurt seeing Nikki, knowing they no longer had a chance at a future.

He just couldn't risk another woman walking out on them. He toed a piece of water-damaged wall. Would it be easier if she left?

George patted his back pocket. "Oh, I forgot my gloves in the truck. I'll be back." He lifted the tall cup to Nikki. "I'm gonna take my time to enjoy my coffee too."

She turned to Adrian. "The other coffee is yours. It's black. Maria said that's the way you drink it." She played with the lid on her cup. "I came up to tell you I won't be here today. I have an appointment at the bank about a business loan."

He stuffed his left hand in his pocket so it wouldn't reach out and trace her jawline or push the loose strands of hair back. Was he wrong? Could a woman who walked out on a child make a lifelong commitment?

Even knowing that about her, he still wanted to hold her close and reassure her it would be all right. Not that Nikki wanted to be held or told he would take care of her. She just wasn't the kind of woman he pictured himself with in the long haul.

In his imagination, when he did give in to daydreams, he saw someone like his mom. A woman happy to take care of the home, cook for her family, iron clothes. He had so many memories of his mom ironing their clothes, even their T-shirts.

Okay, so he could iron his own jeans. And what a waste of time ironing T-shirts. Maybe he wanted a wife who would ride in a storm with him. "Are the rumors true? You're making plans to stay?"

Walking to one of the finished windows, she shrugged. "I don't know yet. I had a business plan made up for Arizona. I've done some research for this area, and I want to talk to the loan officer to see if they see one as stronger than the other." Trimmed fingernails trailed the refurbished wood. "I told Daddy you didn't need me up here getting in your way. It's looking great."

Nodding was the only thing to do. He needed to say something. "Nikki."

She stopped and turned. Waiting, she stood in the middle of the room alone.

Everything in him froze. "How's the knee?" If George had been here, he would've thrown something at him for being so lame.

She tilted her head and her forehead wrinkled. "It's good. The doctor says if it keeps healing at the rate it's going now, then in another month he'll release me to full activities."

"Does he know that full activities for you includes jumping from cliffs?"

She tried to hide her smile by looking down. He took a step toward her. He didn't like the feeling of losing her. It didn't make sense. It wasn't like he ever really had her to begin with.

"The other day, you were honest with me and shared some very private stuff. I just wanted to thank you and make sure you know I'll keep it to myself."

A hand went to her hip. "You didn't even tell George?"

"I'm not sure I'm even talking to him right now. But no. It's not my business to tell."

"Thank you. I hope your problem with George doesn't have anything to do with me." With a glance at her phone, she turned away from him. "I've gotta go. I guess I'll see you around. The rooms are looking great. I can see how it looked in its glory days. 'Bye, Adrian." And just like that, she was gone.

An empty feeling filled his gut. Where did he go from here? Adrian bowed his head and prayed.

One thing he could count on was wood. Old wood talked to him. Head down, he gave his work all his attention. In the morning he would be riding the horses at the Childress Ranch. Life would go on as normal, and if he saw Nikki he'd give her a polite nod.

"Did she leave?" George surprised him. "Did you apologize?"

"I'm working. She had an appointment."

"I moved the Dumpster under the window. So while you talk to the wood, I'll clean up your mess." George stood there like he was waiting for a reply.

Adrian ignored him. He wasn't going to talk about it. Something in his heart hurt and he didn't understand it, and he sure wasn't going to talk to George about it.

Shaking his head, his twin went into the other room. "I can clean up this mess for you, but you have to fix whatever is going on with you and Nikki." A short pause filled with the sound of the old drywall falling. "She's perfect for you. You know you're an idiot, right?"

Yes, but he didn't know what to do about it. It felt like he was seventeen all over again. Trusting someone didn't always work out. "If Nikki leaves, it's not just me, but Mia too. I don't want her hurt."

Boots stomped up behind him. "This is not about Mia. You're afraid of loving her. At least be man enough to admit you're a coward. Stop using your daughter as an excuse. You and Nikki are good together. You're both action people. She could actually keep up with you. You messed up as a teen, but look at the gift you have in Mia. I'm sure Nikki's made mistakes also. Let it go, brother."

Adrian's jaw locked as he dug deeper into the wood. Easy for George to say. He wasn't the one left standing alone holding a newborn baby. All Charlotte had left was a note.

His whole world had collapsed, but he didn't run. He did what he had to do, for his daughter.

After a bit of silence his brother went back to work. Adrian took a deep breath. *God, is it my fear that's making this a problem?* Could he trust Nikki?

Could he trust himself? His attention kept

drifting to the stairs, but they stayed empty. She'd be back. But what if she was done? He wasn't sure how he felt anymore.

She had done a great job of avoiding Adrian all day, but she hadn't been as successful at keeping him out of her head. The bell of the front door chimed as she walked into the hardware store. From somewhere in the back, Joaquin, an occasional Bergmann employee, told her he'd be right out.

"It's just me," she yelled back before taking a deep breath. The smell of old wood and the family business filled her and made her feel at home in a way nowhere else ever did.

Starting a business here where generations of Bergmanns had lived and built a community settled deep in her bones. The idea was moving from whimsy thoughts to real plans.

Stopping at the aisle that housed the little compartments of nails, bolts and screws, she ran her fingers across the front of the boxes. After school, her father had paid her a quarter for each organized box. Would she have kids who would work here one day?

She'd never allowed herself to think about a future with her own family. Living on the edge and staying in the moment kept sadness and guilt away. A stomping sound echoed from the ceiling. Was Adrian still here? She thought he'd be long gone with everyone else.

Joaquin came from the back. "Hey, Nikki. I was about to lock up. Everyone but Adrian has left."

Her family had left her, again. "How am I supposed to get home?" Running ten miles would not have been a problem a few months back. Now everyone would have a fit if she started walking.

"I can give you a ride." Adrian stood at the bottom of the stairs, drying his hands on a paper towel. "I have to drop some supplies off for a project Danica is working on for the teachers at the school anyways."

She groaned. "They did this on purpose, didn't they? Where's George?"

He tossed the paper in the trash. "That's my guess. He had a sudden mysterious task and he offered to pick up Mia. Looks like you're stuck with me."

Joaquin locked the front doors. "I'd take you, but I'm heading to Uvalde. Sorry."

"That's okay. If Adrian doesn't mind me being in his truck, you can go."

"Nikki, I said I'll take you. I have no problem giving you a ride."

"Well, then I'm out of here." The young bull rider whom her dad seemed to have adopted walked past her and winked. "You guys have a good one."

Adrian turned and walked down the narrow uneven steps that led to the back door. She followed. They rode in silence as they drove through town. Really, what did she say to a man who didn't want her around his daughter? Nikki looked out the window. Rejection shouldn't hurt at this point. She wasn't the teen girl desperate for acceptance and love. She closed her eyes.

It still hurt though. It was okay to acknowledge the hurt. That was what the therapist told her.

Acknowledge and move on. There were many people who loved her, including God. She was a child of God. She pressed her forehead to the cool window and watched the fence posts and trees blur as they passed them.

"How did it go at the bank?"

A lopsided smile stretched one side of her face. Adrian had to be the only man she knew who didn't like silence. Why did he have to be so nice? Didn't he know it just led a girl on? "It was good. It looks as if I have some viable options."

"Is one of the options staying here?"

With a sigh, she leaned back and made herself more comfortable. "Yes."

"So are you staying?"

"I don't know." The vibrations of her phone saved her from answering completely. "Hey, Danica. Yes, Adrian's bringing me home." She glanced at him. The tight jaw with a faint shadow of stubble flexed. Easygoing Adrian was not happy. "What? No." She tried to lower her voice. "What makes you think I would ask him to take me to dinner?"

Adrian turned his head sharply and gave her a look that said she was crazy, or her sister was. Either way he thought they were loons. "Why would— Oh. It's not a problem. I'm fine—don't worry about it. We're almost there anyway, and Adrian has the stuff for the school project. I'm good. Okay. Love you."

"What was that all about?"

"She wanted to warn me that Vickie was at the house. She's helping them work on this—" she waved her hand to the bags in the back seat "—project, and stayed longer than planned."

"And that's a problem, why?"

Tilting her head back, she closed her eyes. "Tommy's the father of the baby I gave up for adoption. Vickie doesn't know, and I don't know if I should tell her. I know it doesn't really involve her, but in a way it does. Her kids, anyway. But Danica's being overly dramatic."

The big truck turned into the drive leading to her childhood home. Adrian didn't say anything else until he put it in Park and turned to her. "You know you're right. There's no real reason for you to feel guilty when it comes to Vickie. She knows firsthand what a tool Tommy is. He used you. He used her. If you want, I could take you to dinner. Fred's Tacos is still open."

Oh man, she could kiss him, but she knew he was just being a nice guy. He couldn't help himself. It was his default setting, even when he didn't like her anymore.

Taking a deep breath, she shook her head. "I've faced worse. Vickie doesn't know, so there's no reason to be weird, right?"

He nodded and squeezed her shoulder. "Right."

She helped him get the bags full of wooden letters from the back seat. Adrian followed her through the back door.

Stepping into the kitchen, she first spotted Danica and Sammi at the table. Vickie was walking in from the living room. "The kids have been fed. Now back to work." She stopped in the doorway. "Oh hey, Nikki and Adrian. Danica said y'all were grabbing dinner in town. That was fast."

Nikki made sure to smile at everyone but Danica. Her sister was still trying to play matchmaker. "No, there was a misunderstanding. No big deal."

At least Danica had the manners to look guilty. "I'm sorry we all left you in town, but Adrian was able to bring you home, so it all worked out."

"Yes, very convenient. We also have the bags you asked him to deliver." Putting hers on the table, she ignored her sisters' worried glances. Passing them, she got a couple of glasses from the cabinet and filled them with ice.

Adrian placed his two bags next to the table. "There should be a letter for each teacher's name."

Vickie started digging through the bags, handing some of the wood letters to Sammi, who started going through a bundle of tags with ribbons. "Adrian, these are beautiful. I don't know how you find the time. They're going to love these."

"George, my dad and Mia helped. If there are any that have flaws, I'm sure it's George's fault. If there's nothing else, I need to leave."

In her hands she had a glass of tea for him. What had she been thinking? Of course he wanted to leave. She dumped the ice into the sink. For a moment she looked out the window. He wanted to get out of here as soon as possible. That was the danger of starting to lean on someone for support. She just ended up falling.

Danica came up next to her and turned on

the water. Her gaze darted over her shoulder. She leaned into Nikki. "Did I just make things worse?"

Giving her sister the best let-it-drop look she could muster, she didn't answer. "Thanks for the ride, Adrian."

"Mom!" Vickie's son rushed into the room then froze. His mouth tight as his gaze fell on Nikki. His resemblance to Tommy rolled her stomach. He seemed stressed.

His mother dropped the wood letter she'd been holding and stood. "What's wrong? Is someone hurt?"

He looked at Nikki then back to his mother.

"Seth! What's wrong? You're scaring me." Vickie moved around the table and touched his shoulders.

Clear blue eyes came back to Nikki. "Suzie said we're related. Is it true? Do I have a brother? Lizzy said back in high school, you had a son with my dad."

The world stopped spinning. How did Lizzy know? Her gaze flew to Danica—had she told the twins? Shock widened Vickie's eyes. Her hands covered her open mouth.

"I didn't say anything to her." Shaking her head, Danica took Nikki's hand.

She looked down. Why couldn't she feel her

fingers? Her sister's skin had paled. "I'm so sorry. They must have overheard us talking."

"It's true?" The boy's thin shoulders heaved from heavy breaths. "How old is he? Where is he?"

How did she go from living with a secret for over twelve years to, in a short time, having it unravel? She didn't know what to say. This was not how she wanted people to find out. Especially the kids. She hated small towns.

Sammi touched her back as she walked past her and to the opposite side of Danica. She stopped in front of Seth. "He was adopted by some family members and lives in New Mexico." Her little sister seemed to be the only one with words. "Why don't we go outside? We'll let them talk. I'm sure your mother will tell you everything she learns."

"But I want to know his name. Mom, did you know?" When his mother shook her head, he turned to Nikki. "Does my dad know? Why didn't he tell us? Did you tell him?"

She nodded. "He knew." She looked at Vickie for guidance. She had no idea what to say. Crying was not an option.

Vickie had a hand on her son, but the compassion she saw in her eyes nearly brought her to her knees. "Tommy's a…" Vickie kissed her son's forehead and hugged him, Tommy's son.

"Your father has a tendency to only see what he needs, and he'll do whatever it takes to accomplish his goal. He was that way in high school too."

"But I thought you and Dad dated in high school, so how…?"

Sammi closed the small gap between her and the boy. "Come on, Seth. This is heavy news. I think we need to let them talk. Then you can have all your questions answered." Her little sister, once again to the rescue.

"Seth, you know your father is very complicated. I promise, when we get home I'll answer all your questions. Right now, I need to talk to Nikki alone. Do you understand?"

"Yes, ma'am." He turned to go out the back door, his back stiff.

"Thank you, Samantha." Vickie crossed her arms over her chest, like she was cold. "I don't want him alone right now. His father has put us through so much already."

"I know. If there's anything else I can do, let me know. We'll walk to the barn and look at the new arrivals." Sammi followed the boy outside.

When the door closed, Vickie rushed her and hugged her tight, crying. "I'm so, so sorry. How horrible for you. What did he do when you told him?"

Clearing her head with a couple of blinks,

Nikki wasn't expecting this reaction from Tommy's former wife, the mother of his other children. What did she say? How could she explain why she...? "He said we just needed to wait until he got the recommendation from your father. He needed it to get into Baylor and for a scholarship. He told me you weren't really dating."

Vickie leaned back and nodded. "We weren't. I spent more time with Jake than Tommy. My mother wanted us together, and he had dreams of being president of the United States one day. He thought Daddy could help him get there. You and I aren't the only ones he used."

"When I discovered I was going to have a baby...I thought he'd change his plans for us. I was an idiot. It wasn't what he wanted, but..."

"You thought he loved you enough to make it right."

Nikki nodded. "He was so mad, I got scared. And then he told me to..." Taking a step back, she bumped into Adrian. His hands steadied her.

Tucking her head, she wrapped her arms around her middle. Just like that day, protecting her child. "I couldn't."

"Oh, sweetheart. Of course not." Vickie had her arms around her again, holding her even tighter. Making it hard to breathe. "I'm so sorry. You had to be so frightened, and none of us knew you were going through this. I just want to kick him."

Adrian's comforting touch on the small of her back vanished. Leaving her cold. Once again, he was making sure she was okay even after he put her out of his life. Why couldn't she have fallen in love with him in high school?

"Here, sit." Adrian set the tall glass of tea on the table and pulled out a chair for her. "How's the knee? You've been up and running all day."

Vickie sat in the chair next to her, still holding her hand.

"It's fine." She wiped her face with the back of her hand. When had she started crying? Adrian handed her a tissue.

Danica sat on the other side of her and patted her arm. "It's going to be okay. Everyone who matters knows now, and it's fine."

She didn't dare glance at Adrian. He still stood.

Vickie leaned forward, her fingers interlocked around the tall glass of her iced tea. "What happened next?" She shook her head. "I talked to Tommy almost every day, and nothing. He never acted as if anything was wrong. The only thing I remember is he didn't want to talk about you after you left."

"Probably more of a good riddance than anything else," she answered and her sister sniffled. Adrian sat next to her and patted her shoulder. "He said if I told anyone he'd deny it and start rumors about me." She squeezed Danica's hand. "The twins were younger than me, our grandfather had just passed away, Daddy was going through a rough time with Sheila, and poor Sammi was caught in the middle of all the drama. I didn't want to add to it. I thought the best course of action was for me to go to my mom's aunt. She took care of everything and knew a family who were looking to adopt."

They talked for another ten minutes when Vickie's phone vibrated. "It's Seth. He wants to know if we're done talking."

Danica stood and gathered the glasses. "I hate that he found out this way. I'm going to find the girls and have a chat. Since they never came in, I'm thinking they have a clue what they did caused problems. I'll send Ashley to your car."

After one more hug, Vickie went after her son.

Now she stood in the kitchen alone with Adrian. "Thank you for staying. I know you've had enough drama of your own this week."

He shrugged and grinned at her. "Someone

stayed with me while I was doing the whole Hulk thing. Might as well repay them."

"Did it help? Right now, I'd give anything to jump off a cliff or go over a waterfall."

He laughed. "In my experience, most women attack the shopping malls or cut off their hair."

"You've been hanging around the wrong women."

"I've been told that recently." A low chuckle rumbled from his chest.

She wanted to lay her palm against his sternum and feel the vibrations.

"I need to go. Are you sure you're good?"

"I'm always good." She smiled. "I'll walk you to your truck."

"No need. You should stay and rest."

She crossed her eyes. "I have to move or I'm going to jump out of my skin. It's just a walk to the drive and back. I mean, I might go crazy and make a detour through the garden, but I think I can handle it."

He held his hands up in surrender. "You win. I stand corrected." He opened the door and waited for her to walk through. The world looked as if there was a filter of blue covering everything. In the trees, a few birds sang and hopped around. Without a breeze, the air was a bit sticky.

"Oh. I forgot a bag." Adrian reached into the

back of the truck and held up a bag with more of the letters in it.

"I'll make sure they get it." She stepped close to take it, and when she looked up, she was mere inches from him. Without thought, she leaned forward and touched her lips to the corner of his mouth. He didn't move, so she pressed a little more and started to move in for a real kiss. Adrian took a quick step back.

Heat climbed her neck and burned her cheeks. What was she doing? He'd made it clear there was not a future for them. Swallowing, she stepped back and gave him space. "Sorry."

"No, don't apologize. You just caught me off guard."

She studied her boots. Why was she such a hardheaded idiot? He didn't want her, and now he was going to be nice about it.

He lifted her chin with his knuckle. "Hey, being kissed by a beautiful woman makes me a lucky guy. But right now, there's too much going on. And you're not in a good place."

Being in his arms sounded like the perfect place to her. She shrugged. "Can't blame a girl for trying."

He laughed and shook his head. "You're crazy. I'll see you at the hardware store."

She stood there until his taillights disappeared over the hill. She wanted to smack her head against the stone wall. Why did she always set herself up for rejection?

Chapter Thirteen

Adrian slipped out the front door. The sun wasn't up yet and neither should his family be. It was a perfect morning for working the horses.

"Good morning, Daddy." Mia sat on the side step of his truck with her riding boots on. "Last night you said I could go with you if I was awake and ready."

His sleepyhead daughter, usually dead to the world until sunshine filled her room, was sitting on his truck, ready to go horseback riding. His gut tightened. "How long have you been down here?" He frowned at her.

"I wanted to make sure you didn't leave me."

He'd been thinking of Nikki and hadn't even noticed his daughter wasn't in her bed. He needed to get his head on right. "I said that thinking you'd never be up this early, let alone dressed and ready."

"Yeah, I figured that. I noticed you didn't even try to wake me up. Nikki said if I wanted to ride horses again, I had to prove to you I was serious. I think being up before the sun will do that." She hopped off his truck and walked to the passenger's side. "I left a note for *Tío* George so he'd know I went with you." With that, she climbed into the cab and waited for him.

Nikki? She was still taking advice from Nikki. He shook his head. It could be worse. She could be telling him what a mistake he was making by ignoring his feelings for the hard-headed navy girl.

The trip to the ranch was quiet. Pulling up to the barns, he had to smile. His baby girl, determined to prove she would do anything to get back on a horse, was asleep and drooling against the window. The seat belt being the only thing that held her up.

She'd probably sleep for another couple of hours if he left her here with the windows down. "Mia."

She jumped. "I'm awake. I wasn't asleep."

He laughed. "Right. Come on. The sun's coming up in the next hour, and we have work to do."

"Yes, sir!" She jumped from the truck and followed him to the barns. Jefferson, the ranch foreman, already had the coffee going and smiled at Mia.

"So, we have an extra cowhand today. The leg's all better?"

"I still wear the brace for now, but the doctor told my dad I could ride."

Adrian poured a strong cup of black coffee. "If you take it easy. That means walking. You can saddle Tank."

"Tank! He hardly even walks. I've never seen him trot, let alone lope. He's for babies. Or people that can't ride."

"Or girls who shouldn't be riding at all. Before we ride, there are chores to do. You ready?"

"Yes, sir." Without another complaint, she followed all his orders. By the time the sun started peeking over the hills, his daughter had put in a full day's work without one whine.

"Hey, chipmunk. I'm proud of you. Ready to ride?"

Instantly, she stood taller. "Really? Yes! Can I at least ride Lancelot?"

"No. For you, he'd go all out if you asked, and I want to make sure you stay at a walking pace. If it goes well, we'll talk about promoting you. You stay in the ring, and you wear a helmet."

She nodded as she made her way to the stall where Tank waited.

An hour later, he pulled the young horse he

was working with up next to the old Appaloosa. He knew Mia loved horses, but for her to give up sleep was big. His daughter had loved her sleep from the time he brought her home. He'd always been an early riser. She must have got that from her mom.

"How's it going?"

She sighed. "Slow." He rode along beside her in silence for a while. He remembered the first day he held her. Sleeping, she curled up against his chest. His baby girl had been so tiny, it scared him. She'd been almost three weeks early.

How did they get here with her approaching her teens? He always thought of her as his little girl. He never imagined himself being the father to a teenager.

"What are you thinking about, Daddy?"

"You and your sleep habits. Even as a newborn, you loved your sleep. I was told you would eat every two hours, even during the night. So when you didn't wake up, I would get you out of your crib and try to give you a bottle. You'd glare at me." He chuckled. "When I told your doctor, he said to relax. He told me that some babies liked sleeping all night and I should be grateful. Your mother loved sleeping in late on the weekends."

"But you're up before the sun every day. Were you always that way?"

"Yep. Drove my family crazy."

"Nikki likes being up early too."

He cut her a look.

"What? You have so much in common. What happened?"

"Nothing. We just… It's complicated."

"Did it have to do with my mom coming back? You seemed happy with Nikki until then. Are you freaked out because of what happened when I was born?"

"Mia." How did he explain the mess of emotions in his head when he didn't understand them himself? Everything was so tangled up with his seventeen-year-old self, confusing the past and the present. Was he putting things on Nikki that weren't hers?

"Let's ride out for a little bit." He led the horses to the gate and sidestepped his young gelding to open it. Waiting for Tank to mosey through, he tried to sort it out in a way Mia might understand, but it just gave him a headache.

The morning sun coated the ranch in warm light. Birds darted from tree to tree. He took a deep breath. *God, I'm trying to focus on Your will. Lead me on the path that takes me closer to You so I can be the father, son, brother and man You need me to be.*

He needed to get back to doing morning devotionals. Focusing on God and not his own understanding or anger.

"I read Mom's letter." Mia's voice was soft and low. Like she was afraid of hurting him. Taking a deep breath, he prepared to listen with an open heart and mind. This was about his little girl and her mother, not his wounded pride of being left.

"You did? You didn't say anything." *Okay, good. That sounded casual.*

All he got was a shrug and a few seconds of silence. She glanced over at him, her bottom lip tucked between her teeth. "Do you ever regret having me?"

Pulling his horse to a stop, he stared at her. "Have I ever done anything to make you feel that way?"

"No." She patted Tank.

"You're the best thing about my life. Sometimes we find ourselves on a path we didn't expect, but that can put us on a road to blessings we couldn't have imagined. You're that for me. That's why I named you Mia Valioso, my most valuable treasure. I know it's a bit corny, but I was seventeen and you amazed me from the first glimpse I had of your tiny fist. My heart became yours in a way I wasn't prepared for. You changed my life for the better." The gelding grew impatient standing still. He patted him on the withers. "Let's head back to the barns."

"You named me? I thought you both picked my name."

"No, your mother wanted to call you Brittney Dawn, but when she left, I figured I could call you whatever I wanted."

"Thank you for that. I love my name. And there are four Brittneys at our school. One is in my class, and she might have to move. Her parents are getting a divorce. She's sick to her stomach all the time, worried about the future. They're fighting over her and where she'll go to school. She doesn't want to pick between her parents. It's horrible."

"Sweetheart, I promise you'll never have to pick between me and your mom." He turned the horse back to the barn, holding him to a steady pace so Mia didn't get too far behind. The horse started prancing to the side, resisting the bit. Using the reins, he had him spin to the left on his back heels. They walked circles around Tank.

"I know. It's because Mom let you have me. She didn't fight you. If you think about it, that was a pretty good thing for her to do, wasn't it?"

Wow. Those words hit him hard in the gut. "Yeah."

"I was thinking about it the other night at

youth. We were talking about being wise and how hard it can be to make the right decision. They told us the story of King Solomon. Two women came to him." She looked over at him. "You know the story, right? They were fighting over a baby, and Solomon said to cut the baby in half, so they could both have him. The real mom says no—let her have the baby. A real mother would rather give up her baby than see him hurt. That's kind of what my mom did. Instead of hurting me, she let you have me."

She stared straight ahead. "When we prayed, I thanked God for that, because you're a good dad."

Eyes full of worry, she glanced at him. She needed him to understand. He could see that so clearly.

"In her letter, she said she knew you would take care of me and love me the way she couldn't."

Adrian took a deep breath. His eyes and throat burned. Mia's words wrapped around his heart. *Thank You, God, for this child You laid in my arms. Let me be worthy to raise her.* "You're amazing, and I think you're right about being thankful."

"Daddy, I was thinking I could invite my mother to the July Jubilee, and she could see me ride."

That got his attention. "Who said you were riding in the July rodeo?"

She nudged Tank forward trying to get even with his horse. Tank just flicked his ears and kept going one hoof at a time. "The doctor told you I could start riding again, and if I work at it I figured I'd be ready by July. Nikki said she'd be there too."

"Nikki will probably be back in Arizona by then."

Her shoulders shrugged. "She said she'd be there."

Was she misleading Mia? "Don't get disappointed if she doesn't make it, or your mother, for that matter."

"I know. I invited them, but it will be up to them if they come or not. I know you'll be there, and *Tío* George." She smiled at him.

He laughed when he realized she somehow had got him to thinking about her riding in the rodeo. "Okay, but listen to me. You will be wearing a helmet."

"Daddy! No one wears those at the rodeo!"

"No one else is my daughter, and you are the most precious thing in my life. If you want to compete, you will be wearing a helmet. If you don't want to wear a helmet, that's fine. You just won't ride in the rodeo."

Ha. He wasn't going to fight her over this.

He was feeling rather proud of himself. This was parenting done right. He knew he needed to enjoy this moment because before the week was out, he'd mess up just as big and go back to doubting his parenting skills. For now, he sat up straight. "Yep, sweetheart, your choice. Watch from the stands in your cowboy hat, or run the barrels with a riding helmet."

She sighed. "I don't have to ride Tank, do I?"

He laughed at the expression on her face. He couldn't blame her for the love of speed. She got all that from him. "You can ride Charm or Lancelot."

"Thank you, Daddy!" The smile she flashed him lit up his world brighter than the noon sun. "I can't wait to tell Nikki! She told me if I worked really hard, you'd see that and trust me to ride again. She said she couldn't wait to watch me ride."

"Sweetheart, you know she might not be here. I don't want you to get hurt. You've worked hard to get back on a horse, but you can't make others do what they don't want to do. No matter how much you pray for it to come true."

"I still don't understand why you stopped seeing Nikki."

"Something came up, and it just didn't work out. It happens that way sometimes."

"It happened when Mom gave you the letter. You got all weird."

"I didn't get weird."

"Yes, you did. You were smiling and laughing. Then Mom walked into town and wanted to see me and you got all huffy puffy big bad wolfy." She lowered her voice and scrunched up her face.

"I do not get huffy puffy, and I don't look like that. Nikki wants to live in Arizona, and I want to live here." Maybe he had fallen into a moody place since Charlotte talked to him.

"Would you want to date her if she stayed?"

"I don't want you to get hurt if it doesn't work out."

They walked the horses to the tack room. Mia dismounted with ease and cross-tied Tank between the two poles before slipping off his bridle.

It seemed he didn't have to do everything for her anymore. Now she even carried her own saddle. She was growing up too fast. "I'm glad you came with me this morning. This was good."

She handed him a brush. "Daddy, I understand that people leave sometimes. Just like you said earlier, you can't control other people or what happens, but you can't live in fear of being hurt either. You should date Nikki. I'm going to grow up, and you shouldn't be alone. Plus, I like her better than anyone else that you might date."

She took Tank outside to one of the pastures.

He shook his head as he checked his horse's hooves. Charlotte had given him a gift, and for ten years he had her all to himself. He stood and ran his hands over the powerful muscles of the young horse.

Nikki was strong in so many ways. One of the strongest people he'd ever met. What if she was another gift God had put in his life, but he was too self-righteous to see it? He leaned against the barn wall. *God, I don't know what to do. I don't want to let her go, but I don't want...*

What he didn't want was to be hurt, to be rejected. What was stopping him from loving Nikki? His own wounded pride.

He stood straight and looked out the big barn doors. Mia and Tank could be seen in the distance as she turned him loose. He patted the gelding. "No need to rush, right? I have plenty of time to figure this out. Maybe even a whole month before Nikki decides if she's leaving."

She wasn't going anywhere in the next few weeks. He'd feel it out and decide what to do. He didn't understand why everyone seemed to want him in a relationship. He had everything he needed to be happy.

Chapter Fourteen

Adrian had an extra thump in his chest as he walked through the back door. Nikki would be here. Would she smile at him and avoid eye contact? He didn't blame her for not trusting him after the things he'd said to her when she'd first told him about her past.

Tommy. He growled. Now, there was someone he'd love to…

"Good morning, Adrian! I see you brought a new helper today." Danica stood behind the old counter in the middle of the store. She picked up a bowl full of caramel candies. "What brings y'all in so early today?"

Mia took one of the candies. "We were at the ranch before the sun was up and now Daddy wants to get some work done here." She stood on her toes and leaned forward on her elbows. "I think he wants to see Nikki."

"Mia!" Sometimes he wondered why he couldn't teach her how to be discreet.

Jackie appeared on the upper landing at the back of the store. "She's not here. I'm about to head to the ranch to pick her up. There was something out there she wanted to get before she left for Arizona."

"Arizona?" Blood rushed through his veins. He looked between Jackie and Danica. "I thought it would be another month before she even had to decide if she was going back?"

"Hi, Adrian. Hi, Mia." Sammi came in from the back door. She paused when she saw his face and stared at him. "What's wrong?"

"Nikki's leaving today?" How had he run out of time? She couldn't leave yet. There were too many words he needed to say. He'd wasted too many opportunities. He should've been trying to prove he was worthy of her instead of…

He'd been too stubborn and now he might lose her.

She looked at him in confusion. "Yeah, but—"

"Sammi, I think Adrian might want to go to the ranch and stop her from leaving."

Jackie rushed down the steps. Wrapping her arm around the youngest Bergmann sister. "Just like in the movies we saw last night. He has to rush to the wedding in order to stop his love from marrying the wrong man."

His heart stopped. "What? Nikki's getting married?" This could not be happening. He just realized he loved her. The blood left his legs. He loved Nikki Bergmann.

Sammi shook her head with a frown on her face. "No, she's not getting married, and she's not—"

Jackie squeezed her little sister. "No, she's not getting married. We were just talking how every girl deserves a romantic story where the hero chases her to declare his love for her before it's too late."

"Oh!" A huge grin replaced the confused look on Sam's face. "Like in the second movie, where they all got in the car to stop her from leaving. He apologized in front of everyone." She turned back to Adrian. "Are you going to apologize for hurting her?"

Adrian was getting a headache. "Nikki's not getting married, but she is leaving?"

Danica walked around the counter and joined her sisters. "Yes, but if you asked her to stay, it might be enough reason for her to move back home. Mia can stay here with us so you can go to the ranch in Jackie's place."

"Go, Daddy!"

"Do you think she would accept an apology from me? Would she stay if I asked her?" Air was having a hard time getting into his lungs.

He studied the three women. They nodded in unison, each with a matching smile. Nikki's smile. The smile he wanted to see again, more than he'd thought possible.

He glanced at his daughter. "What do you think?"

She clasped her hands together and jumped. "Yes! Go, Daddy. Tell her we want her to stay."

For the first time in over a decade, the front gate of Forget-Me-Not Ranch stood open, unlocked. Adrian prayed that it meant Nikki would listen to his words.

The road to the cabin was rough as he pushed his truck as fast as he could along the overgrown path. The cabin's door swung open, and Nikki stood in the doorway.

He threw his truck in Park, and it slid a bit in the damp dirt. After cutting the engine, he sat there and looked at her. He was there—now what did he do? What were the words that would make her want to stay and take a chance with him?

The heavy metal car door creaked as he opened it. She frowned at him. He needed to breathe. There was so much on the line. He'd already made so many mistakes.

The song "Take Me Home, Country Roads"

played from inside the cabin. Maybe she was already thinking about staying here.

"Adrian?" Drizzle now dripped from the edge of the roofline. She moved to the bottom step, not seeming to notice the light rain. "What are you doing here? Is everything okay?"

"I heard you were leaving for Arizona." The ground between them took too many steps to close. It was as if the quicksand he'd feared as a child actually made an appearance. Finally putting his boots on the steps, he took her hand and led her to the protection of the covered porch. "Are you sure that is wise? Are you fully recovered?"

He wanted to hit his own head against a brick wall. That was not what he came to say.

"I think I'm well enough to travel." With a frown, she pulled her hand out of his and walked back into the cabin. "I've put it off long enough. I need to go."

Adrian closed his eyes. *God, help me here. I'm messing this up.*

He followed her. "I can't believe it wasn't that long ago I carried you out of the rain." His life had changed that day without him even knowing.

Time ticked, and he had to say the right thing. He had one opportunity to get this right.

The thought of her gone didn't settle right in his bones.

Sweat ran down his spine and beaded on his forehead. He was a mess without a clue of what to do or say.

Nikki stopped at the edge of the kitchen area and turned on her heel. Pride, determination and strength radiated from her as she looked at him with her back straight and her chin high. She seemed to be waiting for him to hurt her again.

"Tell me it's not too late. I was wrong about so many things. All the things I thought I had to give up to be a good father, you brought back into my life."

The frown on her face deepened. "Adrian, what are you talking about?"

It had sounded so good on the neck-breaking drive out here. Now it was all pure drivel. He needed to apologize. "I'm sorry." There, he said it.

Hands on her hips, she narrowed her gaze. "For what?"

Okay, so she wants details. He'd never had a problem with words before. He swallowed. There was so much at stake. "When you first told me about your baby, I didn't respond the way I should have. You were brave and courageous while I acted judgmental and petty."

That got her attention. The hard look was replaced by confusion and maybe doubt. "Thank you? But I'm still not sure why you rushed out here to tell me that. What are you doing here?"

He took a deep breath and looked around the room. It had been cleaned and dusted. The Bible from the closet, the Bible she hadn't wanted to see last time, now sat on the table. Her duffel bag sat on the floor. He was going to have to go all in if he wanted a chance to prove to her that he was serious about a future together.

"I want you to stay. I know I don't have a right to ask you to change your plans for me, but I want a chance at a future together. One that could be better than anything we might do apart." He swallowed and stood there, feeling exposed as she stared at him. "I have to tell you something." What if it scared her away?

"Well?" She lifted her hands. "I have an airplane to catch."

"Yeah. What I need to tell you is…I…" He scanned the room. How to say it? He forced his hands to relax, took a deep breath.

"I love you."

Nikki blinked a couple of times. Not what she'd expected to hear. "And you decide to tell me now? Why?"

He stepped closer to her. "When they told me you were leaving, I had to tell you how I felt before it was too late. Please tell me I'm not too late?"

"Too late? This could have waited till I got back. Now I've got to leave, and we won't have time to discuss this the way it deserves."

He tilted his head as if she was speaking another language. Yeah, she had feelings for him too, but they were too tangled to sort out.

"Can we have a do-over when I get back in a couple of days? We can have dinner and talk about this without all the pressure. You just went from not being able to look my direction to saying you love me. It's a lot to process."

He kept looking at her with confusion clouding his expression. She pushed on, trying to make sense of her own feelings and the words Adrian was throwing at her. "The other day, you made me feel small. Like I wasn't good enough to be around your daughter." She shook her head.

"Now you want me to miss my flight because of three words that might or might not mean anything, so we can talk about a future you're suddenly interested in? What did I miss?"

He walked to her bag and lifted it. Setting it on the table, he looked at her, a crease between his brows. "What do you mean we can have dinner when you get back? I thought you decided to move back to Arizona and make a go at your business."

Now it was her turn to be confused. "No. I'm just going back to wrap things up so I can move to Clear Water permanently."

"You're staying!" His face lit up and, in one motion, his arms went around her, slightly lifting her off the ground as he hugged her. "That's great!"

With her hands on his upper arms, she leaned back and looked at him. "Who told you I was moving to Arizona?" Her eyes narrowed. "Did Jackie send you out here with the idea I was leaving for good?"

Her feet were back on the ground and a cold breeze drifted between them. Adrian moved to the other side of the table. "Sorry. I'm an idiot. Jackie, Danica, Sam and Mia implied I needed to get here as fast as I could in order to stop you." He shoved his hands in his front pockets and looked out the kitchen window. "They were talking about some movie y'all watched last night. Danica said every girl deserves to be swept off her feet and pursued."

She couldn't help but laugh. She bit her lip to control the urge when he scowled at her. "Last night, we watched a couple of Jackie's romantic comedies. They had that British actor in them? I don't remember his name, and I fell asleep during the second one."

"If you're asking me, I have no clue. I'm more into a good Western or action film. Mia's always trying to drag me to one of those chick flicks."

"We can let her go with my sisters while we see a good movie. Romance is overrated. Doesn't happen in real life. Not for girls like me, anyway."

He was back in front of her. "Hey now. That's not true. I just might have run a red light to get here, and I'm pretty sure if Jake had been around I'd have a speeding ticket." His hand cupped her neck, his warm palm pressed against her pulse as his fingers tangled with her loose hair.

His eyes moved as he searched her face. She wasn't sure what he was looking for, but she felt like a deer in a scope. Frozen, waiting for his next move.

"Nicole Bergmann, you deserve to be courted and pursued. Maybe I was sent out here under false pretense, but I know what I felt when I thought you were leaving for good. I had one thought. To stop you, by any means necessary. When will you be back? I want to say these words so you know I mean them. Not just throw them at you as you run by. They deserve… You deserve the time to hear them right."

Her throat was dry. "In two days." Hope could be such a dangerous thing.

"Can I pick you up at the airport and take you to dinner?"

"I don't know." She needed to stay centered and be emotionally strong. Closing her eyes, she took two deep breaths and said a prayer before making eye contact again. "Adrian, I'm at a good place in my life. I'm teaching myself to see my choice for the gift it was. It was the best, for me and my son. Along with his parents. I can't have someone in my life who doesn't see it that way. If you can't respect the choices I made, I won't risk being with you. I really like you. I like us together, but I have to know you're not going to throw that at me whenever you get mad."

One corner of his mouth curled up a tiny bit. "Who says I'm going to get mad?"

She gave him the look.

"Okay, I can't promise I won't get mad, but I won't stay mad. And I'll never hold your past against you. You're so brave. Please, don't be afraid of loving me. You're the kind of woman I want in my daughter's life."

"You want me to stay because of Mia?"

"No." He cupped her face, looking into her bright blue eyes, their lips mere inches apart. "I've loved you since I was thirteen years old, but you were out of my reach. There's a light inside of me that you've brought back." He took a step closer to her and reached for her hand. "I know that sounds corny, but I don't know how else to explain it."

Last week, she had cleaned and aired out the cabin. The smell of citrus still filled the air as she followed him to the once again cozy living room. Her stomach quivered.

Adrian was the kind of man a girl wanted to follow. But if he turned on her? She'd have a harder time recovering from the kind of hurt he could cause.

She needed to keep her guard up. "Adrian, the future I always wanted is becoming a reality, and I won't allow another guy to derail me." Even if it was Adrian. Sadness was heavy in his eyes, and she wanted to take the words back. She didn't want to see him hurt either. "I'm sorry. I think I just need some more time."

He nodded. His fingers caressed her hands, the hands of a working man that could be as gentle as he was strong. She swallowed and waited for him to talk. Adrian De La Cruz wasn't talking. Now she was nervous. "Adrian?"

From under his lashes, he glanced up at her. "Sorry. I want to get the words right. I've recently discovered that what we see as truth is based on our own experiences and the emotions that surround them. Today, Mia went to the ranch with me and rode one of the horses."

"You let her ride? Adrian! That's huge." Why did she want to cry knowing how important it was for Mia to know her father trusted her on a horse again? "She had to be so excited. Are you going to let her ride in the July Jubilee?"

Leaning back a little, he grinned. "She was excited until she saw the horse I put her on. You know him—Tank."

"That's mean."

"She's a trouper and went with it. Yes, I gave her permission for the rodeo, but only if she wears a helmet. She wants you there, and her mother." He let out a heavy sigh. "See, I can listen and be open-minded."

All she could manage was a nod. No man had ever made an effort to change for her. It had always been about their needs and wants.

"What really hit me was a lesson she gave me. While we were riding, she told me about her last Bible study. It's the one where the women are fighting over the baby. You know it, right? Ms. Bible Champ."

"I know it. King Solomon." Where was this going? Free of his hold, her hands rubbed the jeans on her thigh.

"Mia said it made her think of her mom, and the way her mom wrote that I would keep her safe. That a real mother was willing to put her child's well-being over everything else, even if that meant giving them to someone else to raise. Charlotte gave me a gift by trusting me to raise our daughter when she couldn't, but I've been so caught up in all the things I had to give up I didn't see it. In reality, I gained so much more than anything the bull-riding world could have given me."

He reached across and touched her hand. "That's what you did also. I'm sorry if I ever made you feel ashamed. I had no right to judge you. I should have honored the sacrifice you made. The gift you gave to your son's parents."

Unable to sit any longer, Nikki jumped up from her chair. "It's time to go. If I'm going to make my flight, I need to leave in the next ten minutes." She put her mother's Bible in her duffel bag, pausing for a moment to calm her breathing.

A gentle touch on her arm turned her back to Adrian. He stood less than a foot away from her, his hand connecting them.

"Emotions don't have to be bad things, Nikki." He sighed. "May I drive you to the airport and pick you up when you get back? I'd like to take you to dinner so we can talk."

Did she risk it? Everything inside her yelled one word. "Yes."

The pounding of her own heart was so loud, she wasn't sure he heard the whisper. She was going to do this. She was going to allow herself the freedom to love Adrian. He closed the small gap between them.

Hands cupped her neck. The tips of his fingers pressed gently into her skin and his lips met hers. The very core of her being melted.

Closing her eyes, she leaned into him, kissing him back. She didn't know a kiss could make her feel so cherished and loved.

The sun came through the window, caressing her skin. She wrapped her hands around Adrian's biceps to steady herself. All these years, hiding in the dark, she forgot how good the sun felt. Adrian was the sunshine to her darkness.

One last nip at the corner of her mouth and he rested his forehead against hers. "I made a promise to myself not to chase another woman, not to give someone the power to destroy me. Nikki, you keep pulling me into your world. I like it there, and I don't want to leave." He closed his eyes. "I think you already have my heart, and I'd love to prove to you that I can be trusted with yours." His thumbs caressed her cheeks.

She closed her eyes and nodded. "I'm not sure how much heart I have left to give, but it's already yours." She closed her eyes. "That scares me."

The warmth of his breath and smell of soap tickled her senses. He pressed his lips against her hair. "Me too. But I think we can do this. If we both turn everything over to God, we can do this."

He needed to understand she was not looking for a knight in shining armor. "I don't need to be saved by you."

"Oh, sweetheart. Saving you? One of the things I love about you is you don't need saving. But I'd love the opportunity to love you. Will you let me love you? And maybe pull you out of the rain every now and again."

Sand and gravel dried out her throat. She couldn't get a word past them.

Dropping his hands, Adrian took a slight step back. He reached for her hand and intertwined their fingers. "You don't have to say anything now." He glanced over his shoulder then grabbed her bag. "The clock has struck midnight and your time has run out. Your carriage awaits."

"You might have the wrong girl. I'm not a fairy-tale princess."

He winked and marched out the door. A strange noise sounding like a giggle escaped her lips. Horrified, she covered her mouth. That could not have come from her, but when Adrian chuckled she couldn't deny it.

"I like that sound," he yelled back at her. With a swing, her bag was tossed into the bed of his truck. He smiled as she got in the truck. "I guess I owe your sisters a favor now. They've given us almost two hours of uninterrupted time."

"Oh no, you hadn't planned to drive to San Antonio today." She was going to kill her sisters when she got home. Or thank them.

As soon as she was alone, she was calling. Maybe by then she'd know if she was going to kiss them or strangle them. To her horror, a tear slipped over her bottom lashes. She wiped it away and looked out the window, hoping Adrian didn't notice.

She might not have her mother, but God had given her three sisters who would do anything to see her happy.

Adrian's grin softened her hard edges. "No worries. It's an unexpected gift. Time with you. God is good."

"All the time," she whispered.

He laughed as his truck bumped its way down the overgrown path. "Yes, all of the time."

His hand reached for her hands. "Nicole Bergmann, I love you."

The words had never had such true meaning

to them before, but they still scared her a little bit. "Right back at you, Adrian De La Cruz."

He winked at her. Understanding her more than any other man ever had.

Epilogue

Adrian took a deep breath, inhaling scents of the rodeo. He loved everything about it: the smells, sights, sounds and energy that sparked his nerves. Today he was a bit in overdrive. The last few months had been the best in his life, and he thanked God every morning and every night.

He scanned the oak tree grove for Mia and her mother. They had been talking over the internet, and today they met for breakfast. Mia seemed to be taking it all in stride. She was excited when she saw her mother at the rodeo.

Her mother. He was going to have to get used to that and not shudder every time she said the word.

When he left to get the horses ready, he gave Mia a way out, but she asked to stay and visit with Charlotte. Life was shifting, and he had to remind himself it was all in God's hands.

A laugh that lifted his heart came from somewhere behind him. He twisted in the saddle and found Nikki holding her horse's lead, standing next to her father, her great-aunt and the couple who had adopted her son. They had come in for a huge family reunion. A young teen ran up to his father and took some money handed to him before running off with Seth and a few other boys.

The boy looked so much like Seth and Tommy, everyone in town had probably figured it out by now, but no one was talking. Which was pretty incredible, in itself. Hearing her laughter and seeing her happy made his heart feel lighter.

He patted his pocket. The ring suddenly became a heavy weight in his shirt. Everyone in the whole county, her extended family, plus all the visitors from across the country, would be talking soon. Sweat coated his whole body.

When he first thought of ways to propose to Nikki, he knew it had to be big and grand. A way to show everyone how proud he was of her. The stands were packed with people. The reality of what he was about to do set in. If she said no, it could be a major embarrassment.

Plus, it wasn't fair to put her on the spot like this either. She didn't like big emotional hoopla. What had he been thinking? He let Mia watch too many YouTube videos.

He needed to find Danica and Jackie to tell them to call it off.

He'd ask Nikki tonight, at the family dinner. That was a much better idea and still very public.

"Daddy!" Mia stood and grinned at him. He dismounted and led both horses closer.

Mia took the reins of the big gray gelding. Lancelot nickered softly and rubbed his forelock against her, causing her to laugh. He couldn't help but relax at that sound.

"Thank you, Daddy." She turned to her mother. "He also brought Tank and told me I might be riding him. He's super slow."

Charlotte joined them. "I'm looking forward to seeing you ride. I used to love watching your father. Either on a horse or a bull, he was something else."

"I wish I could see him on a bull at least once."

"Oh no, those days are so far behind me, you can't see them in the rearview mirror."

"Before I run the barrels, we have a special show." Mia leaned closer to Charlotte. "Daddy is going to ask Nikki to marry him in front of everyone, right in the middle of the arena. I get to carry a flag."

Charlotte's eyes went big. "Wow."

He glared at his daughter, before turning back to Charlotte. "I'm having doubts about this."

Mia gasped. "About asking Nikki? No!"

"Shh." He glanced over at Nikki and her group. "Not about asking her, just about making it so public."

Charlotte put her hand over her heart. "Oh no. Every girl dreams about a big gesture of love."

"Nikki is not like other women." His gaze went back to staring at the beautiful woman he wanted to make his wife.

"All women want a man that loves them enough to risk embarrassing himself in front of a crowd." Charlotte had a goofy grin on her face.

"Yeah, Daddy. What she said. It's too late anyway. Mr. Miller—" she turned to her mom "—he's the announcer, has the script. And the Bergmanns have the flags."

His stomach rolled a bit.

"Hi, Charlotte." Nikki had walked up behind him. "So are we ready for the exhibition?"

He wiped his forehead. "I was thinking about calling it off."

Mia scowled at him and Charlotte laughed. "I've never known him to get nervous to enter the arena, but then again, I haven't been around lately."

"Daddy's fine. He's worried about me." She crossed her arms and narrowed her gaze.

"Adrian, she'll be fine. I would love to know what exactly I'm doing. Why do you need me to stand my horse in the middle of the arena?"

"Don't worry, I'm not going to be jumping over you or anything crazy, but I do want you to know…if you want to say no to anything, you can. At any time, if you want to leave the arena, you go. I don't want you to worry about me. Promise?"

With a tilt of her head, Nikki gave him a cockeyed look. "Okay."

A phone vibrated. Charlotte pulled hers out. "My friends are here." She hugged Mia. "I'll be in the stands cheering you on." With a grin, she winked at him. "And praying that all goes well with your show. 'Bye, Nikki. I'm sure I'll see you later."

Mia turned her head. "Where are your sisters? They have the flags."

"We have flags? Now I'm really curious. What am I doing with a flag?"

"You don't have a flag." Mia mounted her horse. Before he could remind her, she took the helmet he had looped over the saddle horn and put it on and secured the strap. "You just make sure you're in the center of the arena." She giggled. "I see them at the back gate. This is going to be great!"

He ran his hand over his forehead. What if she hated him for doing this to her?

"Adrian." She touched his arm. "Are you okay? What's going on?"

With what he hoped was a reassuring smile, he shook his head. "It's good. I just hope I didn't mess up. Have you ever done something that sounded like a great idea, then afterward you realized how stupid it was, but it was too late to change course?"

She laughed. "Really? That would pretty much describe my life up to this point."

Should he just tell her?

Frank called his name from the announcer's box. He took a deep breath and tried to calm the craziness in his head.

Nikki mounted her horse. "That's you." She looked down at him as if he had lost all his good sense.

With a hand on the saddle horn, he swung onto Zeta's back. One slight touch of the reins, and she spun on her heels and headed to the arena. Without looking back, he knew Nikki followed on her big palomino.

He leaned over Zeta's neck and ran her into the arena, as fast as she could sprint. They made spirals and figure eights, hitting each flying lead change. Frank introduced him as a hometown boy with some of the titles he won with the

Childress's cutting horses. With barely a touch of the reins, Zeta came to a long sliding stop and started spinning on her back heels. The crowd went wild with cheers and yells.

Coming to a stop, he waved at their enthusiastic audience. His family, even his mother, was in the stands. Charlotte sat with a group of people he didn't know. Everyone from the Childress Ranch was there. He nodded to Mr. Bergmann. Nikki's father tipped his hat and winked. Everyone was there, plus a few thousand others.

Frank introduced Nikki, asking the crowd to show their appreciation for her service to the country. She walked her horse through the deep sand of the arena and waved. Everyone stood and cheered.

Addressing her directly, Frank got her attention. "So, Nikki, I hear you are the star of the show tonight."

With a big smile, she shook her head no and pointed to Adrian.

"What? You mean you don't know why you're out here?"

She shrugged her shoulders, palms up. There were chuckles in the stands. She pointed to the gate behind her. Mia, her sisters, nieces and Vickie Torres were lined up there with their flags. They waved back, but shook their heads no.

"Seems they left you out here on your own. Adrian, do you know what she's supposed to do?"

Swinging his leg over, he dismounted and started walking to her.

"Ladies and gentlemen, I do believe our poor cowboy has a question to ask his sweetheart."

He had never had so much trouble walking in the sand before. He kept his gaze on Nikki. He saw the slight intake of breath. Blood pulsed through his limbs, and he could feel his heart pounding. He turned and looked at Frank.

"Seems our cowboy needs some help with his lady. Mia, can you help your dad out here?"

Kicking her horse, helmet on her head, Mia charged into the arena and ran along the railing. Danica followed her. Jackie, Lizzy and Suzie came next. Vickie was the last to enter the arena. Their flags started flying.

The crowd went wild. His eyes stayed on Nikki. He saw the change in her face as she scanned the flags. He pulled the ring out of his pocket and reached up to take her hand.

This was it. *Please, God, don't let me ruin this.*

Nikki read the flags again. Each flag had one word. Mia's started with *Nikki*. It was followed by *Will. You. Marry. Me?* The last flag carried by Vickie had *Adrian* written on it.

She read them again. They popped in the wind as each horse flew by her. Unable to take her eyes off them, she sat there and stared. Adrian was asking her to marry him in the middle of the biggest public event in Clear Water.

The announcer's voice pulled her attention back to the crowd. "Seems as if our cowgirl's at a loss for the right words. What do you think she should say?"

One word vibrated through the arena and over the hills. "Yes! Yes! Yes!" She looked down. Adrian stood there, holding her hand in his. In his other hand he held a ring.

"She seems to be making our boy sweat it out."

She dismounted and ran her fingers across his forehead, below the rim of his hat. "You're sweating."

"Stands full of cheering people seemed like a good idea on paper. It's kind of noisy and not very romantic. I'm sorry. Someone told me women liked big gestures. This was the biggest thing I could think of." He kept rattling on, but couldn't seem to stop himself. Leaning in closer, she took in his warmth. "Mia and your sisters came up with the flag idea. I just wanted to let everyone know how much I love you and how proud I am of you. I—"

Dry, her throat wouldn't work, so she stopped his words with her fingertips on his lips. Oh no, she was going to cry. She blinked several times, trying to hold back the burn.

Reaching up, he curled her hands into his and kissed each of her knuckles. She was lost in his dark gaze, and the world fell away. She was standing in front of Adrian and he wanted to spend the rest of his life with her. Her, Nikki Bergmann. She shook her head in disbelief.

He pressed her hand against his heart and started talking again. This time she just smiled and listened. She loved the sound of his voice.

"Nikki, there are parts of me I had locked away, but with you I'm fully alive. I've been working on building the perfect home, but it's just a building. Will you build a home with me?" He dropped down to one knee. "Nicole Bergmann, will you marry me?"

"Oh, Adrian."

His breathing became harder. "Nikki?"

She smiled and nodded. "Yes. Yes!"

"Are you sure?" His nostrils flared.

"Adrian De La Cruz, I love you." She couldn't stop the tears this time. The words had never felt so right. "I'll say yes a thousand times if you need me to."

"Once will work." He slipped the ring on her finger.

The world started spinning. Her boots were off the ground. Adrian held her close and spun her in a circle. Throwing his head back, he let out a shout.

Laughter bubbled out of her heart. She wanted to sing and dance.

"I believe that's a yes, people. How about they give us a victory lap with their flag bearers?" The crowd got so loud, they drowned out the announcer.

He gave her a quick kiss. "I think they want us out of here so they can start the bull riding."

She didn't want to let go of him, or this moment. With his hand on her waist, he helped her mount. Normally, she would have bristled at his help in front of so many people, but right now her legs were so weak she needed it. And it had nothing to do with her injury.

Her sisters rode past and grinned. Adrian pulled his horse next to hers and reached for her hand. In step, their horses followed the others around the arena once, then out the gate. He never broke contact with her.

Once out of the arena, they were surrounded. Dismounting, they were swallowed up in hugs and well-wishes.

"Daddy, I told you she'd say yes." Mia ran

from her horse to hug them. "Now I get to have two moms."

"We're so happy for you." Her sisters wrapped her in their arms. People talked and laughed. Everyone was happy. *Happy* wasn't a word she would use to describe her emotions.

Happy was too tame. *Joy* might be closer, but still lacked something.

For the first time in her life, she might actually be in a state of euphoria. How cheesy was that? She couldn't stop hugging people and smiling. Her left hand stayed firmly in Adrian's grip.

He leaned in and whispered low. "How do we get out of here?"

"I don't know. I think we're stuck for now."

A few more people joined them. More hugs and happy tears. Finally, people started drifting off. The bull riders were about to start.

Adrian cupped her neck and kissed the corner of her mouth. "How about next weekend?"

Her brain wasn't working. "What's next weekend?"

He smiled at her and she knew she'd agree to whatever he asked. "Let's get married. We can go to the courthouse and get the license and I'm sure Pastor John can be available."

"Next weekend?"

He tilted his head toward the group standing

behind him. "If we give them too much time, they'll have us releasing live doves." His eyebrows wiggled. "We both love adventure. Why wait? Let's jump."

Glancing around, she saw her sisters and father talking with Mia and George. His parents and sisters were talking with her aunt. They were all smiles. He had a good point. Plus, she liked pushing herself to the limits. Why not? It was Adrian, and she trusted him with her life. More important, she trusted him with her heart.

"Okay."

He hollered and everyone looked at them; even the horses looked as if they doubted his sanity. Hand in hand, they went and told their loved ones that they had a week to plan a wedding. She was marrying Adrian De La Cruz.

God was good, all the time.

* * * * *

*If you enjoyed this story,
look for these other books by Jolene Navarro:*

*LONE STAR HOLIDAY
LONE STAR HERO
A TEXAS CHRISTMAS WISH
THE SOLDIER'S SURPRISE FAMILY*

Dear Reader,

Thank you for taking a trip to Clear Water, Texas, with me. This small town has become my go-to place to visit and Adrian is one of my favorite guys in town. He has been there to help out since the first book and I wanted to see his happy ending. Each story I got to know him a little better and knew I would love spending time with him.

Nikki was new to me. I knew Adrian needed someone who would shake up his world and that's what she did. It was important for me to get her story right for her ultimate gift of love. A story of redemption and forgiveness. We've all made mistakes or trusted the wrong people, but God's love is bigger than anything that can harm us in this world. He uses it all for good. Family, healing and love are all wrapped tightly around this story. Coming from a family of three girls, I loved writing the sister scene. I hope you enjoy Adrian and Nikki's adventure to everlasting love. Find me on Facebook at Jolene Navarro, Author.

Warm regards and blessings,
Jolene Navarro